D1008690

My Mom

and Other Mysteries of the Universe

Clarion Books

New York

Clarion Books
a Houghton Mifflin Company imprint
215 Park Avenue South, New York, NY 10003
Copyright © 2004 by Gina Willner-Pardo

The text was set in 12-point Cantoria MT.

www.houghtonmifflinbooks.com

Printed in the U.S.A.

Library of Congress Cataloging-in-Publication Data

Willner-Pardo, Gina.
My mom and other mysteries of the universe / by Gina Willner-Pardo.
p. cm.
Summary: Eleven-year-old Arlie is troubled by the sudden arrival
of a new girl in school with an uncanny resemblance to Arlie's mother,
a woman who rarely praises her.
ISBN 0-618-43020-2
[1. Mothers and daughters—Fiction. 2. Brothers and sisters—Fiction.
3. Family problems—Fiction. 4. Traffic accidents—Fiction.
5. Schools—Fiction. 6. Theater—Fiction.] I. Title.
PZ7.W683675My 2004
[Fic]—dc22

2004000247

ISBN-13: 978-0-618-43020-8
ISBN-10: 0-618-43020-2

MV 10 9 8 7 6 5 4 3 2 1

To my daughter, Cara, whom I love and admire beyond words,
even after she told me that if we'd been in the same class,
we probably wouldn't have been friends

one

"Arlie!" Mom yelled.

Arlie Metcalfe laid her book down on her chest and propped herself up on her elbows. She surveyed her room, trying to see if anything was out of place, if maybe she'd left her shoes or backpack or markers out in the living room instead of putting them where they belonged. But no, from where she lay on her top bunk, she could see her shoes and backpack and markers, her desk with its orderly array of pens and notebooks, the top of her dresser with its picture frames and her favorite mirror. All her books were arranged from tallest to shortest on the shelves, former home to Arlie's stuffed animals and dolls. Arlie's mom had packed these in boxes and stored them in the garage the summer before. "Dust catchers" she'd called them, and Arlie had nodded, trying not to think of them as real: confused and hurt, wondering where Arlie had gone, why she had abandoned them.

"Arlie!"

Her mom was a neat freak. That was the way she described herself. She liked for everything to be lined up on shelves and hung up in closets. She hated walking into the kitchen and seeing that someone had left a cereal bowl in the sink. She would yell at Arlie to clean up after herself if it was hers, or shake her head and rinse it out herself if it was Michael's.

1

Michael was only six. But Arlie had had to rinse out her own bowls since she'd been old enough to hold her own spoon.

"Arlie!" Mom's voice was closer now; her heels clacked on the hallway floor. "Are you in your room?"

"Yeah!" Arlie called back.

The doorknob turned.

"Arlie!" Mom said. "Where have you been?"

Mom was tall and thin, the kind of woman who tucked her shirt into her jeans and washed her white sneakers the second they got dirt on them. She had chin-length dark brown hair that always looked as if it had just been combed, and eyes that were a surprising blue. Even now, after so many years of looking at her, Arlie got surprised by those eyes. You didn't expect them, under all that dark hair.

"Just lying here," Arlie said.

"Haven't you heard me calling you?"

"Yeah, but you always come anyway."

Her mom sighed and glanced around the room. "Did you put your dirty clothes in the hamper?"

"Yep."

"And did you sweep under the bed?"

Arlie sighed, knowing that it wouldn't make any difference if she said yes or no. Her mom would still sound the same.

"Yes."

"How about your homework? Are you done with that yet?"

"It's only four-thirty, Mom. I was reading. I can do homework after dinner."

"You know the rules, Arlie. How many times do I have to tell you?"

Arlie could hear it in her mother's voice: a slide up from talking to yelling. "But I don't see why—"

"Arlie. Don't start with me," Mom said. "I'm losing my mind today." Almost to herself, she added, "What little is left of my mind." It was one of her favorite expressions.

Arlie forced herself to keep silent. She was always trying to explain how unfair the rules were, even though she knew her mom wasn't going to change them. Her mom was strict about rules.

Mom crossed her arms on her chest and leaned toward the bed. "What are you reading?"

Arlie held up the book. "*Heidi*. Mrs. Rubio said it's good. She said she read it five times when she was a kid, and it always made her want to drink warm milk."

Mom wrinkled her nose.

"Because they drink it in the book. With cheese and bread. Anyway," Arlie said, "it's about a little girl and a shepherd. It's good."

"I don't think I ever read *Heidi*," Mom said. "Does it take place in Holland?"

"Switzerland."

"I'm mixing it up with *Hans Brinker*, I think," Mom said. "Now that was a good book. You should read that."

"Are there animals in it? In *Heidi* there are a lot of goats." But Arlie was thinking that her mother was always saying "should," always letting her know that she had picked the wrong thing to like.

"I'll see if I can get it at Cody's on my lunch hour," Mom said. "I think Michael would love it."

As if on cue, Arlie heard a crash in the next room.

"*Mom!*" Michael wailed.

"What, honey?" Mom called.

"My *block tower!*"

"Michael," Mom said. "Come in here, please. I don't like all this yelling." But she was smiling at Arlie, as if they were both thinking the same thing: that it was cute when he did it.

A moment later, Michael trudged into the room, dragging his feet as if they were almost too heavy to hoist off the ground. "My *tower!*" he moaned.

He was thin and tall for his age, with wavy brown hair and big, soft eyes that made grownups smile and coo, as if they were looking at kittens or a panda.

"What happened?" Mom asked.

"It broke!"

"Fell down, you mean," Arlie said. Irritated, she added, "It's just blocks. Build it again."

"I liked it the way it *was*."

"Build it the same way," Arlie said.

"I can't. I can't remember where everything went."

Arlie thought about arguing with him—If you liked it so much, then how come you can't remember how it was?—but didn't. He looked sad, really sad, something Michael almost never was. Usually he was giggling and full of jokes that Arlie didn't think were funny but that made her laugh anyway.

"I'll help you," Mom said, gazing down at him. "We'll build a new one. It'll be neat."

Michael nodded, looking weary but satisfied, and trudged out of the room.

Arlie imagined her mother on her hands and knees, fitting blocks together, not even noticing the dust balls under Michael's bed. "Hey, Mom," she said. "What were you calling me for?"

"Oh, my gosh. I almost forgot. Mrs. Sweeney called."

Arlie's heart sank. She and Belinda babysat for Jesse Sweeney when Mrs. Sweeney needed to pick up groceries or get the dry cleaning or just sit on a park bench by herself. Arlie got the feeling Mrs. Sweeney needed to do a lot of sitting. Jesse was a handful.

"She's got to run to the store and the post office and the bank. She was wondering if you and Belinda could be there in twenty minutes," Mom said.

Belinda Friedlander had been Arlie's best friend since first grade. She was lucky because she had freckles and a swimming pool and a mother who baked tomato-parmesan bread every Saturday and didn't care if everything was put away. Her dad had died when she was just a baby, though, which wasn't so lucky. Out of habit, Arlie suddenly thought, Frelinda Biedlander. She and Belinda were always doing that.

"Oh, Mom—"

"Listen, Arlie. You begged me to let you and Belinda babysit for the Sweeneys. You *begged* me. For summer art classes, you said. You *had* to take Introduction to Architectural Drawing, you said."

Arlie was the only eleven-year-old she'd ever heard of who had to pay for her own summer classes. All the other kids' moms cheerfully paid for things like Fun with Clay and So You Want to Speak Japanese? But Mom told Arlie that she'd better get used to paying for the things she wanted. And that it was fine with her if she stayed home all summer. She could clean out the garage and take care of the lawn.

"And now that Mrs. Sweeney is depending on you, you never want to go over there," Mrs. Metcalfe was saying.

"Honestly, Arlie. It's time you learned a little something about being responsible."

"It's that rotten Jesse Sweeney," she said. "He throws food at us."

"Four-year-olds are like that," Mom said. "You and Belinda just have to show him who's boss."

Arlie sighed again, even though the thought of Architectural Drawing this summer had begun to thaw her heart a little. She had wanted to be an architect before she even knew the word for it. In preschool, she had drawn houses instead of trees and people. She would stamp her foot and scowl when her father admired her blanket-draped constructions. "It's a *house,* not a fort," she would say.

As she got older, she still loved to draw pictures of houses she'd like to live in someday: two-story houses with flower boxes at the downstairs windows and steep roofs; cottages set in tangled, overgrown gardens; modern houses, all wood and glass, built into the sides of mountains. Not like her house now, which looked like everything else on the street: drab and dull, with square rooms off a long, dark hallway.

Someday Arlie would live somewhere beautiful and different, in a house that people stopped their cars to look at, a house that smelled like good things cooking and sounded like laughter. And people would drive away thinking that children who lived in a house like that sure were lucky; they probably had parents who did everything for them, loved everything about them, and always made sure they were happy.

Now, though, it was only February, and summer classes seemed far away. Arlie lay back down on the bed and pulled *Heidi* over her face. "What about my homework?"

"You can do it over there. Come on, Arlie, get going.

Belinda will meet you there. Mrs. Sweeney is waiting."

Arlie didn't move. From underneath her book, she heard her mother say, "I'm not going to tell you again."

Just those words—and the way she said them—were enough to let Arlie know she meant business.

"*Okay.*" She sat up, then slumped. A part of her still hoped that if she took her time, her mother would change her mind about making her go. She hoped, but she knew better. Her mother never changed her mind.

"Arlie. Now." Mom glanced in Arlie's mirror and patted her brown hair, already neat and smooth.

Slowly Arlie crawled to the ladder, turned around, and climbed down.

"Babysitting isn't just about you, Arlie. It's about keeping your promises. Being dependable."

"I know, I know."

"Don't 'I know' me. And turn around when I'm talking to you."

Arlie turned around. "Sorry."

Mom glanced at her watch. "Don't keep Mrs. Sweeney waiting."

She and Arlie sighed. Arlie thought that it sounded as if their sighs had come from the same body.

"*Mom!*" Michael said from the doorway.

"Please don't whine, honey," she said, but she allowed him to tug her down the hall to his room.

"I know what you mean," Belinda said. They were standing at the counter in the Sweeneys' kitchen; she was pouring orange juice into a cup and concentrating on not spilling. "My mom is always telling me stuff, too."

"It's not the same," Arlie said. "Moms always tell kids what to do." She opened a cupboard and pulled out a box of cereal bars. "This is different."

Belinda was her best friend in the whole world, but Arlie still couldn't tell her what the problem really was. That she could do everything the way she was supposed to—read all the right books, dust every stick of furniture, wash every dish in the house by hand—and still nothing would be right.

"I like your mom," Belinda said. "She makes good enchiladas. She smells nice."

Other moms yelled about putting away markers or emptying wastebaskets, but it wasn't the same. Arlie wasn't sure why. Maybe because once in a while they said nice stuff, too.

All she said to Belinda was "She uses a special soap. With cucumbers in it."

Just then they heard a thud in the TV room, followed by a piercing wail. Arlie and Belinda looked at each other and rolled their eyes.

"Great," Arlie whispered. In a louder voice, she called, "What's wrong, Jesse?"

More sobbing, which, now that Arlie thought about it, sounded pretty fake.

Still. Babysitters couldn't take chances. Arlie and Belinda raced out of the kitchen and down the back hallway.

"What, Jesse?" Belinda called as they ran.

Panting, they stood at the door to the TV room. The room was a mess. Magazines, sections of a newspaper, and a plate covered in doughnut crumbs littered the coffee table. One of the couch cushions lay half on the floor. Off to one side of the TV, a Chutes and Ladders board had been unfolded. A plastic basket that had been full of Legos was over-turned.

"Jesse?" Arlie called, not seeing him at first.

"Here," he said, his voice shaking.

He lay between the couch and the coffee table. He was large for a four-year-old, with curly black hair, pale skin, and chubby knees streaked with dirt. He wore red shorts, a red and white striped T-shirt, and blue sandals that stuck to his sweaty soles. Sometimes, just looking at Jesse's fat pink toes made Arlie feel like she might throw up. She worried that there was something wrong with her, that maybe she would never be able to love a baby of her own. Weren't girls sup-posed to love babies, even if they did cry a lot and have nasty feet? She was afraid to tell Belinda, afraid that Belinda would think she was weird. So she just kept quiet.

"I fell," Jesse whined.

"What happened?" Belinda asked in the sweet voice that she used when making Barbie ask Ken why he'd gotten fired.

"I fell off," Jesse said. He sniffed. "The couch." His face crinkled up as if he might start to cry again.

"Oh, come on, Jesse," Arlie said, impatient with Belinda's niceness. She reached out a hand. "Here. Stand up."

Jesse lay right where he was, shaking his head no against the carpet.

"Maybe he's hurt," Belinda said.

Jesse peeked at her hopefully.

"He's not hurt," Arlie said.

"I am *so*," Jesse screamed, beginning to cry in earnest. He stamped his feet against the floor. "I am *so* hurt!" he yelled.

"You are not," Arlie said, sighing and feeling guilty, as though it were her fault Jesse was lying on the floor.

"I'm hurt!" he yelled again. "And my mom says I get a brownie when I'm hurt."

Arlie and Belinda shot each other *aha!* looks.

"Not so close to dinner, honey," Belinda crooned. "You know you're not allowed to have treats."

She sounds like a real mom, Arlie thought. Like the way Mom had sounded with Michael when he was four, even though Michael wasn't the kind of kid who cried for no reason.

Jesse pushed out his lips and tried to look pathetic. "But—"

"Come on, Jesse," Arlie said firmly. She walked over to him, knelt down, hooked her hands under his armpits, and pulled him to his feet. "You're fine. Quit faking."

"I'm *not* faking!"

"Well, quit crying, then. Just . . . quit it. Just behave."

Real tears were running down Jesse's cheeks now. He stamped his feet again.

"He's having a tantrum," Belinda whispered in awe.

Jesse routinely had tantrums, but they were always amazing to watch, like TV news pictures of tornadoes picking up trailers as if they were tin cans.

"Well, at least he's having it standing up," Arlie said. Inside, she was a little afraid. What if Mrs. Sweeney came home? What if Jesse told her they'd been hitting him or making fun of him?

She forced herself to imagine the long, hot summer with nothing to do but mow the lawn and stack cardboard boxes full of books and baby clothes on the garage shelves.

Putting up with Jesse Sweeney was worth it, she thought, imagining instead the air-conditioned cool of the community center, the feel of a number two pencil in her hand, the clean, square outline of a building taking shape on the paper before her.

"We'd better get him to stop, I guess," she said.

Belinda sat down on the couch and took hold of Jesse's hands.

"Come on, sweetie," she begged. "Don't cry. Please."

Jesse wrenched one of his hands away and wiped his cheek.

"I don't like her," he said, looking at Arlie. "Make her go home."

"Jesse—"

"She's mean," Jesse said. "And she smells."

"Hey!" Arlie said. "What's that supposed to mean?"

"Arlie!" Belinda whispered. She turned her head so only Arlie could see. "He's four!" she whispered.

"Well, I don't care. I'm telling Mrs. Sweeney," Arlie said, although she felt a little stupid, threatening to tattle on a four-year-old she was supposed to be taking care of.

"Why don't you just go back to the kitchen?" Belinda suggested. "I'll handle it."

"Yeah," Jesse wailed, rubbing his eyes. "Let her handle it, why don't you?"

Arlie felt humiliated. "I'm just as much in charge as you are," she said to Belinda.

"I know, I know," Belinda said, nodding. "But you're making him mad."

Arlie was silent, watching as Belinda rubbed Jesse's fat little fingers against her own cheeks. It was true. Arlie didn't know how to calm Jesse down. She only made everything worse.

"Want to play Chutes and Ladders?" Belinda asked Jesse.

"I go first!" Jesse yelled, his tears suddenly gone, his eyes creased into smiley slits.

"You get the pieces out," Belinda said, rising from the couch, "and I'll get us some orange juice."

Jesse rummaged in the game basket. "Tell her to leave us alone!" he shouted without turning around.

Out in the kitchen, Belinda said, "I wasn't trying to leave you out. Honest."

"I know," Arlie said. "I guess I'm not very good at this babysitting stuff."

"Yes, you are," Belinda said. "If there was a fire, you'd be good at calling an ambulance."

"I know," Arlie said. "It's being nice I have trouble with."

"You're nice." Belinda smiled. "I couldn't be best friends with someone who wasn't nice."

"Thanks," Arlie said. "But it's easy being nice to you. You don't throw Cheerios at me or say I smell."

"You don't smell."

"Are you sure?"

Belinda opened the refrigerator door and put the orange juice back on the top shelf. "Positive."

Arlie felt a little better.

"It just takes patience," Belinda said.

"How does Mrs. Sweeney stand him?"

"She loves him," Belinda said. "He's a good kid, underneath it all."

"He's *awful*."

"But if he was your kid, you wouldn't *notice* that he was awful."

Arlie didn't answer, trying to imagine what it would be like to have a mother who didn't notice you were awful.

At dinner, Dad said, "Mom and I have some exciting news."

Arlie looked up from her Brussels sprouts with interest.

"You're not having a baby, are you?" Michael asked.

"Michael!" Mom said. "What makes you think that?"

"Because Ryan Beasley's mom is having a baby."

"So?" Arlie said. She brushed some mashed potato off a Brussels sprout, then speared it with her fork and popped it in her mouth. "Just because one lady's having a baby doesn't mean everyone is. It's not like catching a cold."

"I just don't want Mom having any more babies," Michael said. He eyed the two Brussels sprouts on his plate with loathing. "*I'm* the baby."

Arlie loved her brother. He was capable of doing all the rotten things that gave little brothers a bad name—like throwing your favorite stuffed animal out the car window on the family trip to Lake Tahoe, or imitating everything you said until you screamed for him to shut up and then got in trouble. But somehow, Arlie always forgave him. There was something about him. She knew he never meant to be crummy. He just wanted to see what would happen. He'd even said so once, when she'd found him emptying her body glitter into the toilet. She'd yelled, but later, in her room, she'd laughed until her stomach hurt.

Everyone loved Michael.

"Of *course* you are, sweetie," Mom cooed. "And I'm *not* having a baby."

"As a matter of fact," Dad said, "I'm going on the road."

Arlie's father was a musician. He played the drums, and usually he played close to home: in nightclubs and bars, at street fairs and weddings and bar mitzvahs. Arlie loved to watch her dad play. When he soloed, people clapped and hooted and yelled for more. Sometimes, Arlie thought she would explode with pride. She hated when he went away.

"How long?" she asked, at the exact same moment that Michael said, "Can I come?"

"About a month," Dad said. "It's a warm-up band."

"What's a warm-up band?" she asked. She imagined her dad playing drums in a blizzard, the audience pink-cheeked, huffing on their hands.

"It's a band that plays *before* the band that everyone really wants to see," her dad explained.

To Arlie, this sounded depressing. Out of the corner of her eye, she could see her mother reach across the table to hold Michael's hand.

"How come they don't want to see you?" she asked.

"Well, they do, but they really want to see the main act."

"Can I come?" Michael asked again.

"Who's the main act?" Arlie asked.

"Vertical Fruit," Dad said proudly.

"Vertical *Fruit?*" Michael shrieked.

"They're very good," Dad said. He looked insulted. "One of their guitar players used to play with In Your Face."

This meant nothing to Arlie, but she knew from the way her father said it that he was happy, and she wanted to be happy for him. "Cool, Dad," she said.

"It's a stupid name," Michael said, but Arlie could tell

that he didn't really mean it, that he was being disagreeable because he had figured out that he wasn't going along.

Arlie knew how he felt. A whole month with just Mom seemed like an awfully long time.

But then she heard her father say, "The exciting thing is that Mom's coming with me."

Arlie perked up a little. This was something different. Usually when her dad went on the road, he was gone only for a couple of days. Mom just stayed home.

Michael wiped his napkin across his mouth. "That's not fair," he said.

"How come you're going?" Arlie asked. Her mom didn't play anything. She didn't even like musicians all that much, except for Arlie's dad. She called them deadbeats.

Mom said, "To keep an eye on things. Make sure the motel reservations don't get fouled up. Make sure everyone gets paid."

"What about your job?" Arlie asked. Mom was an office manager in a dentist's office.

"I have some vacation time coming."

"Won't Dr. Feldenkraus be mad?"

"He'll understand. Business is business."

"Mom *has* to come along to make sure of things," Dad said. "You know how she is." He winked at Arlie.

Arlie smiled at him. When other dads imitated Groucho Marx or Jack Nicholson, she only pretended to laugh: secretly, she wished they would just stop. But Arlie's dad was really funny, the way he did impressions and teased her friends about how they talked and whether they liked any boys yet. Most dads wouldn't have been able to get away with it. He was the kind of man grownups wanted to be friends with and kids wanted to hang around. "Your father is a very charming man," Arlie's mom was always saying. "But not much of a businessman."

"What about us?" Arlie asked now. "Who's staying with us?" The possibilities in being left alone began to glimmer. "Can I go to Belinda's?"

"What about me?" Michael yelled. "I don't like my friends. Where will I go?"

"What do you mean you don't like your friends?" Arlie asked.

"I don't like the way other people's houses smell. I don't like going to the bathroom at Walter's. There's no lock from the time when Walter shut himself in there until his mom said he didn't have to take tap-dancing."

"You're not going to Walter's, and you're not going to Belinda's," Mom said. "You're both staying with Isabelle."

Isabelle was Arlie and Michael's aunt, Mom's sister, only they never called her Aunt Isabelle. She was too young to be somebody's Aunt Isabelle. She was only twenty-three, just out of college, and working at the wildlife museum. She was Arlie's favorite person in the whole world.

"Hooray!" she said, spitting a Brussels sprout across the table by accident. Michael laughed and Mom said, "Oh, *Arlie!*" But Arlie was so pleased about Isabelle that she almost didn't notice her mother's irritation.

"Isabelle's got the coolest apartment I've ever seen," she said. "Ferns and flowers on all the tables and purple rugs and pots hanging from the kitchen ceiling instead of packed away in drawers. And a Ouija board instead of Monopoly. And crystal balls. And fortune-telling cards."

She pretended not to notice Dad rolling his eyes. He

loved Isabelle, but he always said she was kind of a kook.

"And car seats instead of chairs!" Michael added.

Arlie knew he was talking about Isabelle's leather couch.

"I love how she makes scrambled eggs for dinner and spaghetti for breakfast. And she always has cool things in the refrigerator, like pudding cups and leftover macaroni salad with no olives," Arlie said.

"And locks on the bathroom door," Michael chimed in.

"How long will you be gone?" Arlie asked.

"A month. A little longer if the gig in Santa Fe comes through," Dad said.

"That's almost a year," Michael said.

Arlie was too happy even to correct him. "It'll be our vacation, too. Even though we're still in school," she said.

Dad reached for more mashed potatoes.

"You'll hardly miss us," he said. "You won't even know we're gone."

Taking her plate to the counter, Arlie thought about saying "I *will* miss you." But then she saw her mom watching Michael, who was pulling leaves off a Brussels sprout with his fingers. If it had been Arlie doing it, Mom would have said something about not playing with food.

She set her plate in the sink without saying a word.

two

Mom and Dad ran around like crazy people getting ready for their trip. Dad had to buy new drumsticks and get the tires on the car rotated. Mom had to teach the woman from the temporary employment agency how to book appointments and talk to patients about how much money they owed Dr. Feldenkraus. People were always calling the office to complain about their bills. Arlie tried to imagine what her mother said to help them, but she couldn't. At home, Mom always said Arlie didn't have anything to complain about.

The night before her parents left, Arlie lay on the floor by their bed as they packed. The room looked different from down there: big and unfamiliar, the ceiling like an empty space that everyone had just forgotten about. The bedside table still had a price sticker taped to its underside. The floor beneath the bed was as sparkling clean as all the others in the house.

"Hey, Lacey, how many pairs of socks, do you think?" Dad stood over his open suitcase, looking completely confused.

"All of them," Mom said without hesitation. She stood behind him, one fist on each hip, looking around the room. Her suitcase, packed and zipped, stood in the hallway.

"Really? Do I need that many? They take up space."

"Just take them. Otherwise we have to make more trips to the Laundromat."

"Good point." Dad hated Laundromats. "What about a tie? Do you think I'll need a tie?"

"Bring one. You never know."

Dad nodded, as if he'd never have figured that out on his own. Which was weird, Arlie thought. When Mom stayed late at her office, Dad made elaborate dinners for Arlie and Michael: meat loaf topped with slices of bacon; Caesar salads with homemade croutons; turkey with the stuffing cooked inside, not in a separate pan. After he'd cleaned the kitchen, he'd help Arlie with her homework. "Compound fractions!" he'd say, the way other people said "Ice cream!" In college, Dad had won an award for being the best in math. He was actually very smart and good at figuring things out.

Before he was a musician for real, Dad had just played drums for fun. Back then, he was an accountant. He figured out people's taxes, which he'd thought would be like doing math and getting paid for it. He and another man, his best friend from college, had had their own office, with a secretary who answered the phone by saying, "Metcalfe and Dean. How may I help you?"

Being an accountant had been okay, Dad said, until Frank Dean had stolen all the money. "From under my nose," he said, making Arlie think that there had been piles of bills stacked on every desk, and Mr. Dean had just kept slipping them into his pockets without anyone noticing.

After he had figured out about the stealing, Dad didn't want to be an accountant anymore. The fun had gone out of it, he told Arlie. "What's the point if it isn't any fun?" he asked. Arlie agreed with him. She was glad he was a musician, because music made him happy, and he liked being on-stage, the center of attention. But she knew it had hurt his feelings having a friend who'd stolen from him. Now the only person he trusted was Mom. She helped him keep his schedule straight and hire other musicians and made sure he got paid the right amount of money after every gig he played.

"Arlie?" Mom said, interrupting Arlie's train of thought. "Have you brushed your teeth?"

"Not yet."

"Well, for heaven's sake, go do it. What are you lying around for?"

"Can't I wait a few more minutes?" Brushing her teeth meant bedtime, with the lights out.

"No. It's after nine. Go."

From the dresser, where he was rummaging through his sock drawer, Dad looked back at Mom. "Come on, Lace. It's our last night."

Mom sighed. "Well, get off the floor, then. Honestly. It's filthy down there."

It's cleaner than most people's kitchen tables, Arlie thought, but she hauled herself up and flopped onto the bed.

"Ten minutes," Mom said. "No more."

Arlie nodded against the pillow on her dad's side of the bed. A school night. Her mom was strict about bedtimes. Michael had been asleep since eight.

Dad dropped the socks he was holding and slapped his hand against his forehead. "Oh, man!"

"What, Dave?" Mom asked.

"My suit," he said. "It's at the cleaners. I forgot to pick it up."

Mom shook her head and began to head toward the

bathroom. "I'll pick it up tomorrow morning after I drop the kids off at school."

"Are you sure?"

"No problem," Mom said, disappearing into the bathroom. "Did you pack your shaving stuff?"

Arlie let her fingers stray over the bumps of the chenille bedspread. Without the unforgiving floor beneath her, she'd suddenly grown sleepy. "Dad?"

"I'm leaving it out. So I can shave in the morning," Dad called. To Arlie he said, "What, pumpkin?"

"When you went bankrupt, was Mom mad?"

Dad pulled balled-up socks out of the drawer and lobbed them into his open suitcase. "Not mad, exactly," he said, smiling. "But not thrilled, either. Definitely not thrilled."

I'll bet, Arlie thought.

"I think she was scared about not having enough money, and how we were going to get by, and what was going to happen next," Dad said. "But she also felt bad for me, because I'm the one it happened to."

Arlie liked talking to her father because he really *talked* to her. He didn't try to hide bad news or pretend that something scary really wasn't. If he saw a dead cat in the road, he didn't tell Arlie that it was taking a nap. He just told her not to look.

"Mom felt *really* bad for me," he said.

"I guess," Arlie said. It was hard for her to believe him, because when bad things happened to *her*, like getting five wrong on a spelling test or spilling sugar on the kitchen counter, Mom didn't seem to feel bad for her at all. She just seemed mad.

"Pumpkin—" Dad was still smiling at her, but in a sad

way. "She . . . asks a lot of us. But—" He paused. "She loves us very much."

"I know," Arlie said.

"Arlie!" Mom called from the bathroom. "Brush your teeth!"

Ten minutes. On the nose.

Did her mother love her? Arlie didn't know. Sometimes she thought her mother was embarrassed about being emotional, that she just couldn't show Arlie the love she really felt. She wasn't embarrassed with Michael, though, or Dad. Was it something about Arlie herself that got in the way? Did Mom think she wasn't pretty or smart or funny enough? How come other girls got to write jokey e-mails to their moms, or play Scrabble without keeping score, or get ice cream after school just for fun, when it wasn't a special occasion? Things Arlie wanted to do and knew she never would.

Her father loved her, though. She knew that much for sure. And most of the time, that was enough.

Arlie's parents were leaving at five in the afternoon. School that day seemed interminable. Even Mrs. Rubio's usually interesting ideas weren't enough to distract Arlie.

"Too bad they're not flying. Then you could go to the airport," Belinda said during Quiet Talking. Mrs. Rubio let kids talk to their desk groups while they did their workbooks. "I love thinking about where all the people in the airport are going." She sighed. "The only places I've ever been are Mount Rushmore and my grandma's cabin at Silver Lake. And we always drive."

"I've been to Lake Tahoe and the Grand Canyon and

Disneyland. And to Portland for Great-Aunt Ruth's funeral," Arlie said. Then, so it wouldn't sound like bragging, she added, "I've always wanted to see Mount Rushmore."

"It is pretty cool," Belinda said. "Theodore Roosevelt's nose is big enough to stand up in."

"Who'd want to stand up in some guy's nose?" Warren Rutherford asked. He sat in the desk group with Arlie and Belinda, along with Jeremy Sanchez. Mrs. Rubio always tried to make sure there were two boys and two girls in every group.

Warren was small and skinny and wore sneakers with no socks and big, baggy shorts, even in winter. Once he wore his favorite T-shirt—gray, with a drawing of Albert Einstein playing an electric guitar over the words SCIENCE ROCKS—fifteen days in a row, until Mrs. Rubio sent a note home to his mother. Warren always acted as if he knew everything, but Arlie liked him anyway, because he didn't care what anybody else thought.

"Nobody actually stands up in it," Belinda said. "It's just that if you wanted to, you could."

"But who'd want to?" Warren said.

"Nobody. I just said." Belinda sounded irritated. "You can't even get up there. It's illegal to climb around on their faces."

"I'd do it," Jeremy said. "I'd climb in there and pick boogers out of his nose."

Arlie hated Jeremy. All he cared about was basketball. And he only laughed when someone said a bad word or made a mistake.

"Shut up, Jeremy," Arlie said. "You are so disgusting."

"I'd get a whole backpack full of giant boogers," Jeremy said. "And I'd flick them at you."

Arlie and Belinda rolled their eyes at each other. Warren half laughed, but Arlie knew he didn't really think Jeremy was funny, either.

"Jeremy," Mrs. Rubio said. She was right behind him. Arlie had noticed Mrs. Rubio was good at that: appearing out of nowhere, hearing what she wasn't supposed to hear. It was like magic, the way she was just suddenly there. Arlie couldn't understand it.

"I'd find something else to talk about if I were you," Mrs. Rubio said. She had a way of looking at you over her glasses that made you think you were going to disappear in a little puff of smoke, like a rabbit in a magician's hat.

"Okay," Jeremy said. He pretended to be cool, but Arlie knew that inside he was just as scared of Mrs. Rubio as they all were.

For a while, they worked in silence. Arlie wrote in her workbook. She loved school, except for PE and Mrs. Hale, the school secretary, who was supposed to take your temperature if you didn't feel well but instead just made you lie on a cot in another room so she wouldn't have to breathe any of your germs. Part of why Arlie loved school was because of Mrs. Rubio. Even though she could be scary, she was also funny and told interesting stories about when she had lived on an ostrich farm in Australia. Also, school was the best place to hang out with Belinda and Xenia, her other best friend. Xenia's full name was Xenia Iolanthe Zeckendorf, just because her mother had liked the way it sounded. Arlie couldn't even imagine what it would be like to have a mother like Mrs. Zeckendorf.

Mrs. Rubio's classroom was different from all the others. Some of it looked just like any classroom: student work on the walls, blackboards, a bud vase with a rose on Mrs. Rubio's desk. But there was space reserved on one wall for pictures: Mrs. Rubio in a black wetsuit, about to explore the Great Barrier Reef; or sitting on her Harley in the middle of a Kansas wheat field. The classroom clock was in the shape of a motorcycle; everywhere, there were bumper stickers and snow globes and pennants collected from her travels. A big T-shirt was pinned above her desk. It read, IF YOU CAN READ THIS, MY HUSBAND MUST HAVE FALLEN OFF.

Usually workbook time was easy for Arlie, but today she just couldn't concentrate.

"Anyway," she said, as though someone had interrupted her, "Isabelle and Michael and I are going to say goodbye and then go back to her apartment. We have to stay there because she has a pet tarantula and Mom won't let it in our house."

Belinda and Warren looked horrified.

"Really? A tarantula?" Jeremy said.

Arlie nodded. "Elizabeth," she said. She couldn't help noticing that Jeremy was looking at her with newfound admiration.

"The only person I know who lives in an apartment is my uncle Floyd," Warren said. "His bed folds into the couch."

"Sleeping on the living room floor might be fun," Belinda said. "Maybe she'll let you watch TV all night."

"There's no TV," Arlie said.

"No TV in the living room or no TV at all?" Warren asked.

"At all. Isabelle doesn't believe in it."

"Doesn't believe in TV?" Jeremy shrieked.

"Jeremy," Mrs. Rubio said sternly. "I'm not going to tell you again."

"How can you not believe in TV?" Jeremy whispered. "It's not like the tooth fairy, or aliens."

"She just doesn't," Arlie said. She felt proud of how different Isabelle was, and of shocking Jeremy. "She says TV is toxic."

"What's that mean?" Warren asked.

"Like poison. She says TV destroys your brain cells."

"I like TV," Warren said.

Actually, Arlie did, too.

"Isabelle says anyone with a pulse can think of something better to do than watch TV," she said. She smiled. "Anyone with a pulse" was one of Isabelle's favorite expressions.

"Like what?" Jeremy asked.

"Play games. Bake bread. Once she even told my fortune."

"How does she do that?" Belinda's eyes were wide.

"All different ways. With tea leaves. Or by looking at the lines in my palm." Arlie scratched the tip of her nose with the eraser end of her pencil. "Isabelle knows all kinds of ways."

"Okay, everyone. Workbooks closed, please!" Mrs. Rubio called from the blackboard.

One of the things Arlie liked about Mrs. Rubio was that she always said please, even when she was ordering you to do something.

"I need everyone's best attention," Mrs. Rubio was saying. "I need to talk to you all about a very special class project."

Arlie put her workbook away and sat up straight, hands folded on her desk. This sounded important.

"As you all know, our classroom has adopted the residents of the Leisure Valley Retirement Community," Mrs. Rubio said. "The residents loved getting to know you at our pancake breakfast in October. They so appreciated the Thanksgiving dinner you made for them. And Mr. Cronkite said your rendition of 'A Holly, Jolly Christmas' was the best he'd ever heard. Yes, Ben?"

"We didn't really adopt them," Ben Shively said. "When you really adopt someone, you bring her home to live with you."

Ben's little sister May-Ling was adopted.

"That's right, Ben," Mrs. Rubio said. "When we say we've adopted Leisure Valley, we just mean we like to visit them."

Arlie especially liked Mr. Cunningham, who had become her special friend at Leisure Valley. He was eighty-four years old, just like Arlie's grandpa, and still had all his own teeth. He had arthritis, so to keep his hands from getting stiff, he painted pictures and made things out of clay. He had made a mirror for Arlie for Christmas. Arlie had set it on her dresser, and she looked in it every day when she brushed her hair.

"Next Christmas I'll make *you* a mirror," she'd told him.

Mr. Cunningham had shaken his head. "You don't look in mirrors when you're eighty-four," he said.

"Because you're old?" Maybe it was too awful, seeing wrinkles and blotches and hair growing where it shouldn't.

Mr. Cunningham had leaned in close. He smelled like peppermint. "I know what I look like *without* a mirror," he'd said meaningfully.

"You mean you've memorized yourself?"

"I mean I know what I *really* look like, on the inside," he'd said. "My face just gets in the way."

Arlie had wanted to ask more: did he mean he knew what his heart looked like, pounding; his blood, pulsing through his veins? And what if he got a piece of food stuck between his front teeth? Wouldn't he want to know? But she had simply nodded and thought that maybe she'd make him a picture frame instead.

"Anyway," Mrs. Rubio was saying now, "in April, we are going to put on a play for our friends at Leisure Valley. That's only a month and a half away, so we have a lot of work to do."

Arlie loved plays. She and Belinda and Xenia had been putting on plays at recess since second grade, when they'd gotten sick of the sandbox and all the playground equipment. But they'd only been pretending: they hadn't had a stage or costumes or props, and no one to watch them, except for some of the first-grade girls who got carsick on the swings and didn't have anything else to do.

She raised her hand. "Which one?" she asked.

"It's called *Who's Minding the Store?*" Mrs. Rubio said. "It's about a young boy who runs away from home because he doesn't want to work at his grandparents' fruit stand."

Rats, Arlie thought. "Are there any good parts for girls?" she asked.

"Please don't call out, Arlie," Mrs. Rubio said. "There are plenty of good parts for everyone. In fact, I will pass out a cast sheet with a description of each character. You may decide which part you'd like to try out for. Next week we'll have auditions."

Warren raised his hand. "Can I be the young boy?" he asked.

"You'll have to try out," Mrs. Rubio said. "Everyone will get a copy of the script. You'll have a few days to memorize some lines for the auditions. Everyone will be assigned the part that suits him or her best."

Jeremy Sanchez raised his hand. "Do we have to be in it?" he asked.

Mrs. Rubio folded her arms on her chest

"You most certainly do, Jeremy," she said. "And I'd like you to work on your attitude, please."

Arlie wondered what Mrs. Rubio would say about Jeremy's attitude if she knew that he called the place Seizure Valley.

"Okay," Jeremy said reluctantly. "Only why do we have to do a play about a dumb old fruit stand?"

"It isn't about a fruit stand. It's about a boy's adventures away from home," Mrs. Rubio said. "It's about learning to value what you sometimes take for granted."

"Why can't we do something about basketball?" Jeremy asked.

"There's more to life than basketball," Mrs. Rubio said. "Perhaps it's time you found that out, Jeremy."

Jeremy slid down in his seat and sighed. Arlie heard him whisper "Dumb old fruit stand" under his breath, just to let the desk group know that Mrs. Rubio hadn't won him over. She and Belinda looked at each other again. Arlie knew they were thinking exactly the same thing: that Jeremy Sanchez was a huge pain in the neck. And that "stuit frand" sounded much funnier than "fruit stand."

Mom and Dad and Michael and Isabelle were in the car— which was already packed full of suitcases and her father's drum kit—waiting for Arlie when she got out to the school parking lot. She squeezed in the backseat next to Isabelle, who gave her a quick hug and a kiss on the top of her head. "How's my partner in crime?" she whispered.

Isabelle was taller and thinner than Mom; most people wouldn't have been able to tell they were related at all. She had curly red hair that hung below her shoulders and was always getting caught in her dangly earrings.

"You're too old for long hair," Mom was saying. "You look like something the cat dragged in."

Isabelle laughed. "Jeez, Lace, you sound like Mom!"

"I don't see what's so terrible about a nice, neat bob," Mom said, patting her well-combed hair.

"Nothing, if you're fifty-five years old," Isabelle said, laughing and tossing her head, her earrings jangling against her neck.

"And you sound like you're wearing a cowbell," Mom said, barely smiling. "It's a wonder the kids don't call you Bossy."

Isabelle snuck a look at Arlie. "Who's the bossy one?" she whispered. She and Arlie dissolved in giggles.

"What?" Mom asked. "What's so funny, you two?"

"Nothing," Isabelle and Arlie said together, as if they were the sisters.

Arlie leaned close to Isabelle and inhaled. Isabelle always smelled like a vanilla milk shake. Arlie loved that about her, and her thin, flowery skirts and long, freckled arms. Arlie loved everything about Isabelle. She was going to be just like her when she grew up. She would wear sneakers with chiffon dresses and listen to Aerosmith in the morning and Mel Tormé at night and do yoga and name her plants and take baths. And she would never be on time or make lists or tell anybody to do anything over.

"How was school?" Isabelle asked as Dad pulled into traffic.

"Okay," Arlie said. "We're putting on a play for the people at Leisure Valley."

"Oh, fun!" Isabelle said. "I loved plays. I was Dorothy in *The Wizard of Oz* in sixth grade."

Arlie tried to imagine Isabelle's long hair caught up in pigtails. "Did you have to sing?" she asked.

"'Somewhere over the rainbow,'" Isabelle sang in a pretend opera singer's voice. "I really stank."

"I could never sing in front of anybody," Arlie said. "Our play is called *Who's Minding the Store?* There's no singing in it. I don't think."

"What part are you playing?"

"We have to try out. Maybe the grandmother. I'm not sure."

In the front seat, Mom checked her watch and said to Dad, "This traffic is atrocious. And we really need to get on the road by five if we're going to make Northridge at a reasonable hour."

"What's Northridge?" Arlie asked.

"A university. First stop on the tour," Dad said.

"Who's the main character?" Isabelle asked.

Somehow, around Isabelle, Arlie always felt as though what she was talking about was the most important thing.

"Some boy," she said. "Petey. No one's named Petey in real life."

"Pee-pee?" Michael screeched.

"Petey. Pee-tee," Arlie said carefully.

"Try out for him," Isabelle said.

"Arlie's gonna be Pee-pee?" Michael asked, collapsing in giggles.

"I don't want to be a boy," Arlie said, trying to ignore

him. "I want to be the grandma. Except I don't know how to be someone old."

"Sure you do. Just pretend you're all wrinkly." Isabelle twirled a lock of hair around one finger and scrunched lower in the seat.

"I can't. I'm *not* wrinkly."

Dad braked hard and everyone lurched forward. "Dave!" Mom cried. "For heaven's sake! Not so fast!"

"That's why they call it acting," Isabelle said.

At home, they tumbled out of Mom and Dad's Saturn and stood awkwardly in the driveway. Arlie saw Isabelle's beaten-up van at the curb. She couldn't wait to drive away.

"Go on inside, Arlie," Mom said. "I put your suitcase and sleeping bag by the front door. And grab Michael's, will you?"

Arlie ran inside. The house, always immaculate, seemed cleaner still, and silent, as though it were the middle of the night and everyone was asleep. The curtains were drawn. Arlie glanced around, saying goodbye. It was weird to think that nobody would be living there for a whole month. She picked up the suitcases and headed out the front door, glad to be leaving it all behind.

On the driveway, Mom was kneeling down so Michael could get his arms around her neck. "Why can't I come?" he whined, his voice cracking. Mom wiped his cheeks and touched her forehead to his. "It won't be long," she whispered.

Arlie set the suitcases down on the sidewalk. "Thanks, bunny," Isabelle said, hoisting one and then the other into the back. "Hop in."

"I've got to get the sleeping bags," Arlie said, running up toward the house again, grateful not to have to watch Mom and Michael anymore.

Back outside, a sleeping bag under each arm, she was suddenly anxious in a way she hadn't expected. Would she be homesick? Would she miss her house, her street, her parents? Her father's pancakes on Sunday morning, in the shapes of dinosaurs? The way the light looked on the living room rug around four-thirty in the afternoon, when she started getting hungry for dinner? It would be funny to be homesick when she was still at school every day, sitting at her regular desk and listening to Mrs. Rubio. Suddenly, she wasn't so sure about all the fun she was going to have. She felt something—a shiver, a gnawing on a single nerve—that made her look up and down the street, as though something terrible were headed her way.

Just then, Dad came up to her, arms outstretched. He hugged her hard. "I love you, pumpkin," he said.

"I love you, too," she whispered back.

He released her after a moment and went to kneel before Michael, who was kicking at a patch of ivy. "Hey, big guy," he said, pulling him into his arms.

It never bothered Arlie to watch her dad hug Michael, or kiss him, or throw him a ball, or snuggle with him in front of the TV. He did those things with Arlie, too, so somehow it wasn't so hard to share him.

Mom came over and gripped Arlie's upper arms in her hands.

"Don't forget what we've talked about. Your homework. Not staying up too late. Being helpful to Mrs. Sweeney."

"I know, Mom."

"And I really need you to help Isabelle look after Michael."

"Okay."

Mom went on about making sure to wear clean clothes every day and not getting too close to other people's hair, in case they had lice. Arlie nodded and tried to move her arms. "Now, what else?" Mom said.

"Don't talk to anyone who's got automatic weapons slung over his shoulder. Don't eat anything, in case it's been poisoned. Draw the shades if anything resembling a meteor is falling out of the sky," Isabelle said.

Mom let go of Arlie's arms and looked at Isabelle. "Ha, ha."

"Well, jeez, Lacey, they're with me! It's not like they're going to be roaming the rain forests of Borneo with a canteen and a slingshot."

"I just like to remind her." Mom lowered her voice, but Arlie could still hear huffiness. "It doesn't hurt to be reminded."

"Mom! I *know*," Arlie said.

"Come on, guys. Give them a kiss and go, already," Isabelle said. "Let's get this show on the road!"

Arlie extended her arms and rested her head against her mother's shoulders. She felt Mom's lips on her hair and her hands on her shoulder blades: the barest outline of a kiss, a shadowy hug.

"Honey," Mom said, and for a split second, Arlie's heart thudded, until she realized that her mother had meant her dad: she was nodding toward the Saturn. Reluctantly, Arlie backed away.

In a moment, they were gone with a flutter of waves and

backward glances. Arlie and Michael and Isabelle watched until the Saturn turned the corner. Michael sniffed and wiped his nose with his sleeve.

"I hate drums," he said.

Dinner was a special treat: huge plates of French fries at Mel's and chocolate milk shakes for dessert. No hamburgers, because Isabelle said that thinking of dead cows made her lose her appetite. When Michael asked what about a vegetable, Isabelle told him that ketchup was made of tomatoes. Arlie stuffed three fries into her mouth at once and felt giddy with the pleasure of not following her mother's rules.

After dinner, they went to the corner drugstore and looked at magazines. Michael wanted to buy one about motorcycles, but Isabelle said it was more fun to look at everything than to have to decide which one to spend money on. They riffled through magazines about golf and movie stars and fancy houses and snowboarding until the man behind the counter started giving them dirty looks. Then they ran out to the van.

Arlie couldn't wait to get back to Isabelle's apartment and set up her sleeping bag. "It's like camp," she said as Isabelle backed into a parking space a block from her front door.

"Without mosquitoes," Michael added.

"Kind of," Isabelle said, putting on the brake. "Only no campfires in the living room. And absolutely, *positively* no peeing in the bushes."

Arlie and Michael laughed. Arlie thought how every day for the next four weeks would have Isabelle in it, and laughed again, just for the fun of it.

***

But that night, she couldn't sleep. Her sleeping bag was warm and cozy and smelled like Belinda's dog, Crocodile, who slept on it when Arlie spent the night at the Friedlanders'. And Isabelle had left the bathroom light on, so the living room was full of reassuring shapes and shadows. At her feet, Michael snored lightly, hardly loud enough to be heard. Still, Arlie couldn't close her eyes, couldn't let herself go.

It was late when she rose from the floor and tiptoed into Isabelle's bedroom. The bedside lamp was still on. Isabelle lay in the middle of her quilted bed, surrounded by pillows, a lacy blue shawl thrown across her shoulders. In the lamplight, her hair glowed like fairy-tale flax. On the bureau, Elizabeth lay motionless in her glass cage.

"What, bunny?" Isabelle asked, looking up from the magazine she was reading. "Can't sleep?"

"I'm not tired," Arlie said.

Isabelle patted the mattress at her side. "Sit next to me, then. Just sit here while I read."

Arlie climbed onto the bed and settled herself in close against Isabelle. Instantly, she felt warm and sleepy and safe. She rested her head on Isabelle's shoulder.

"What are you reading?" she asked.

"A terrible article. 'How to Get Thinner Thighs.'"

"You don't need thinner thighs."

"I know. I'm dying of boredom. Quick, ask me something so I don't have to read another word."

Without thinking, Arlie said, "How come Mom's the way she is?"

Isabelle laughed. "People just are the way they are, I guess. She's always been that way."

"Did she boss you around when you were little?"

"She was a lot older than I was. She went away to college when I was a little girl. So she wasn't around much."

"Did she babysit you?" Arlie had asked all this many times before, but it was comforting to ask again.

"Sometimes. Her favorite thing for us to do was take all the toys out of my closet and dust them."

"She still does that," Arlie said sleepily. "I hate that."

"It was better than watching TV all afternoon," Isabelle said. "I knew it was her way of telling me she loved me."

Arlie sighed. "Why couldn't she just say it?"

"She *was* saying it." Isabelle leaned her head sideways until it touched Arlie's. "In her own way," she added.

After a moment, Arlie asked, "But didn't you want her to say it the regular way? With words, I mean?" Her voice came out a whisper.

She could feel Isabelle pulling the sheet and quilts over her legs and plumping a pillow behind her shoulders. Arlie scrunched down under the covers until her head lay on the pillow. She heard the springs creak as Isabelle arranged herself, then leaned toward Arlie and planted a soft kiss on her forehead.

"Some people can't," Isabelle said.

"Why?"

"I don't know," Isabelle said, flicking off the light. "It's a mystery."

three

When Arlie woke up the next morning, she knew instantly that something was going to happen.

"Something *big*," she said as she helped Isabelle make breakfast. "Do you ever get that feeling?"

"All the time," Isabelle said, taking asparagus out of the refrigerator. "Every day."

"No, but really. Something *major*. Is that for breakfast?"

"Yeah. Get the coleslaw, will you, bunny?" Isabelle filled the teakettle with water. "How'd you sleep?"

"Really well," Arlie said. "I didn't wake up once. I didn't even dream."

"That you *remember*," Isabelle said. "You always dream."

"I had a big dream," Michael said, rubbing his eyes as he set a jar of peanut butter on the kitchen table. "I was in this jungle, and I was all alone except for Walter, and there was this giant python—"

"Green or black?" Isabelle asked.

"Green, I think."

Isabelle nodded. "That could be important," she said.

Guiltily, Arlie realized that she was always telling Michael to shut up about his dreams.

She turned her thoughts back to the day ahead. No tests that she could remember, or assemblies, or field trips. Still, she was sure that something was going to happen.

". . . and I pulled out this gun and—" Michael was saying.

"Hey, Isabelle," Arlie said. "Is it an instinct when you're sure something's going to happen and you don't know why?"

"You interrupted me!" Michael yelled, spitting part of his peanut butter sandwich.

"Well, I *had* to. Your dreams never end," Arlie said, looking Isabelle's way for support.

Isabelle pointed a stalk of asparagus at Michael. "A pistol or a rifle?" she asked.

"Rifle, I think."

"Okay. Hold that thought." Isabelle sat down at the table and looked at Arlie. "Yeah, that's instinct. It's a feeling. It's knowing something," she said, crunching her asparagus.

"Like how birds know about flying south," Michael said.

He really is a smart little kid, Arlie thought. Even if he does have dumb dreams.

"Trust your instincts," Isabelle said.

Arlie closed her eyes and forked coleslaw into her mouth. Did she really feel something? Was it really there?

Yes. There it was again. A knowing. Strong and clear, like a light that had been left on. She opened her eyes and finished her breakfast happily. Knowing for sure. Knowing like a bird.

There was a new girl.

"From West Virginia," Belinda said as they waited for the morning bell to ring. "I heard Angela Bordman telling a fourth grader."

Angela Bordman's mother worked in the office, taking attendance. Angela got to know everything first.

"West Virginia's one of those states that if you don't have a relative who lives there, you'll never go," Belinda said.

"West Virginia," Arlie said. "What's her name?"

"Casey, I think. I wonder if her father's a coal miner."

"Why?"

"Remember in fourth grade? The social studies book said West Virginia had a lot of coal mines."

"Yeah, but it also said California had a lot of farms and movie studios. And our parents aren't farmers or movie stars."

"I read once that if you take your middle name and your street name and put them together, it would probably be a good movie-star name. Mine would be Estelle Hamlin," Belinda said.

"Mine would be—"

"Ellen Vallecito. I know. Isn't that beautiful?"

The bell rang. Arlie and Belinda ran to line up, promising each other to ask everyone what their movie-star names would be. *Ellen Vallecito,* Arlie thought dreamily, and then remembered that today they would find out more about the play for Leisure Valley. A big day, she thought. I knew it.

By the time Mrs. Rubio had led them to Room 22, Arlie and Belinda had learned that Angela Bordman's movie-star name was Marie Hunsaker, Warren's was Edwin Sweet, and Jeremy's was Milo Brook. Xenia Zeckendorf's was Iolanthe Third, which didn't work at all, and really depressed her, and Chris Olivera wouldn't tell his middle name. Arlie was so busy finding out everyone's movie-star name that she forgot about the new girl until Mrs. Rubio cleared her throat.

"Class," she began, "please welcome Casey Lane."

Everyone clapped and looked around. Arlie finally spotted her sitting near the front in a desk close to Mrs. Rubio's.

She was pretty, with white skin and very dark chin-length hair parted in the middle. She was wearing a dress, which made her look old-fashioned, Arlie thought. Maybe girls wore dresses in West Virginia. In California, in fifth grade, they mostly wore jeans.

She looked familiar, like someone Arlie had already met. Impossible, she thought. I don't know anyone from West Virginia. Then she noticed Casey's eyes, a sharp, glittering blue like her mother's. That must be it, she thought, shivering a little, as though a cool breeze had suddenly blown through Room 22.

"Casey's from Morgantown, West Virginia, isn't that right, honey?" Mrs. Rubio said, looking encouragingly in Casey's direction. Casey nodded. Maybe she's shy, Arlie thought. She probably doesn't like Mrs. Rubio making such a big deal about her.

If Arlie were new, that's how she'd be feeling.

"Who'd like to ask Casey some questions?" Mrs. Rubio said.

Belinda raised her hand. "What's your dad do?" she asked. Belinda was always curious about dads, since she hadn't known hers.

"He's a construction worker," Casey said.

Like Grandpa, Arlie thought.

Ursula Bartels wondered if Casey had any brothers or sisters. Casey shook her head no. Gillian Facher asked what Casey's mom did. "She's a secretary," Casey said. Her voice was low and surprisingly strong, not whispery at all. Arlie felt a funny shiver in her spine. The shy kids she knew usually did a lot of whispering.

Warren raised his hand. "Who's the governor of West

Virginia?" he asked. Everyone laughed. Arlie and Belinda shot each other looks. Warren could be so weird.

"I don't know," Casey said. She sounded ashamed, as though she were supposed to know everything anybody asked her. Looking at Mrs. Rubio, she added, "I can look it up, though."

"That's not necessary," Mrs. Rubio said.

On an impulse, Arlie raised her hand. "This may sound funny," she began. "But what's your middle name?"

She was thinking that telling Casey her movie-star name would be a good way of making friends. Also, she was hoping Mrs. Rubio would tell them what *her* movie-star name would be.

"I don't have one," Casey said.

Arlie was disappointed. "Oh," she said. The only other person she knew who didn't have a middle name was her mother.

Mrs. Rubio was ready to move on.

"Let's tell Casey about the play we're going to be doing for Leisure Valley," she said. "Also, I have more information about the parts you can try out for. Have you ever been in a play, Casey?"

"I used to put on plays at my old school," she said. "I directed them, actually."

It wasn't shyness. Not the way Arlie was used to shyness. Maybe just something quiet and grown-up. How could she not be shy, on her first day at a new school? Arlie tried to imagine being new. She imagined her tongue like a block of cement in her mouth, too heavy to move.

"I like directing best," Casey was saying.

Mrs. Rubio passed out sheets of paper. "This is the cast

of characters in *Who's Minding the Store?* There are parts for everyone, but some of the parts require more speaking. I want you to think about this while you decide what you'd like to try out for. You'll have to memorize your lines, so some of the parts will be a bit more work."

Arlie and Belinda nudged each other under their desks. They were both good at memorizing, and they both wanted big parts.

"I'm trying out for the biggest girl part," Belinda whispered.

"Me, too," Arlie whispered back.

There were twenty-three parts, just the number of kids in Mrs. Rubio's class. But a lot of the parts were for things like "village woman" and "town folk." Arlie guessed they didn't have much to do.

There was Petey, and the grandparents, and Charlie and Sam, listed as "Petey's friends." There was an innkeeper, a peddler, a shoemaker, and a washerwoman. Arlie raised her hand. "Can the innkeeper be a lady?" she asked.

"I don't see why not," Mrs. Rubio said.

"Well, what about the washerwoman? Can she be a boy?"

Mrs. Rubio studied her copy of the cast list and adjusted her glasses on her nose, which was what she did when a kid found a mistake she'd made.

"Good point, Arlie," she said.

"*I'm* not being a woman," Jeremy Sanchez said to no one in particular.

"Let's all change 'washerwoman' to 'washer*person*,'" Mrs. Rubio said, making a note on her cast list. She looked at the class and smiled. "'The times, they are a-changin'.'"

"'Washerperson' doesn't sound very *village*-y," Arlie said.

"You're the one who brought it up," Jeremy muttered. "Keep your mouth shut for a change, why don't you?"

"'Washerperson' sounds fine," Mrs. Rubio said. "This is a very *modern* village."

Arlie glanced over at Casey, who was studying her list intently, and wondered what part she was going to try out for.

At lunch, Arlie and Belinda and Xenia were about to sit on their favorite bench when they noticed Casey alone by the side of the school.

"It's hard being new," Belinda said, and they all nodded.

Belinda went over to Casey, and in a few moments they both turned and headed toward the bench.

"That's Xenia and that's Arlie," Belinda said, pointing.

"That's a pretty name," Casey said, looking right at Arlie, who blushed.

"What part are you trying out for?" Arlie asked.

Casey sat on the bench and opened her bag. Without meaning to, Arlie found herself trying to see inside. You could tell a lot about a person by what she brought for lunch.

"I haven't decided yet," Casey said. "Maybe the grandmother."

"That's what we're all trying out for," Arlie said. "The grandmother's the best girl part."

"I wish Mrs. Rubio had picked a play about a *girl* running away from home," Xenia said.

"But it has to be a boy," Belinda said. "His friends are boys. He wants to be a farmer."

"Girls can want to be farmers," Casey said.

"Yeah, but this was in olden days. Girls didn't want to be farmers back then. They just wanted to have babies and make butter," Arlie said.

"Or they wanted to live in New York and have a carriage and take ocean liners to France. But they married farmers and got stuck," Xenia said.

"And anyway, this boy runs away from home. Girls couldn't run away from home back then," Belinda said. "There was too much danger."

Casey took a bite of her sandwich. Ham and cheese with mustard, Arlie noticed: ordinary, what lots of kids brought.

"Girls could run away if they really wanted to," Casey said. "I think it would be a more interesting story if the main character was a girl."

Once Casey said it, Arlie found herself agreeing. She didn't feel like saying so, though.

"But if it is a boy, then maybe a boy should play him," Casey said.

"I wonder if the grandma will have to wear orthopedic shoes," Belinda said. "My grandma wears them. Maybe I can borrow hers."

"My aunt Isabelle says if you're a good actress, you should be able to be a grandma just by *imagining* orthopedic shoes," Arlie said. "That's why they call it acting, she says."

Casey shrugged. "Just because *you're* imagining orthopedic shoes doesn't mean the audience can."

"My aunt says, and she really knows. She was in *The Wizard of Oz*," Arlie said. She felt a little defensive. Who was Casey to think she knew everything?

Casey smiled. She had a mysterious smile. "That's neat, I guess."

Maybe they say "neat" in West Virginia, Arlie thought.

It was weird. She felt as though she would do or say a lot to get Casey to smile. It wasn't that Arlie liked her all that much. She'd said that stuff about directing, which might mean she was bossy and conceited. And she had argued about the orthopedic shoes.

But there was something about her.

"Your aunt. In *The Wizard of Oz*. Was she Dorothy?" Casey asked.

Arlie nodded. "Even though she wasn't a very good singer," she added.

"Dorothy should be a good singer," Casey said.

"Well," Arlie said after a moment, feeling a strong urge to defend Isabelle, "she's an *okay* singer."

"Dorothy should be better than just okay," Casey said.

As they finished their lunches, Arlie was thinking that people who said "should" all the time were pretty hard to get along with, no matter how old they were.

"She's nice, don't you think?"

"Who?" Arlie asked.

"Casey." Belinda fumbled with the zipper of her backpack as she looked for a bag of chips left from lunch—something to tide them over while they waited for her mother to pick them up after school.

"I can't tell yet," Arlie said.

"What do you mean?"

"Nothing. I don't know. It's just—"

"What?"

Arlie didn't know how to explain. She liked Casey, as far as she could tell. Casey wasn't falling all over herself trying to make people notice her, something Arlie found admirable. She liked putting on plays, which made Arlie think they might have something in common. Even her mysterious smile made her seem wiser, more knowing, more grown-up, maybe, than the other girls Arlie knew. It made her hope that Casey liked *her*, which was somehow different from liking Casey herself.

"I guess I just want to wait and see," she finally said.

Belinda laughed and tore open the bag of Cool Ranch Doritos she had found. "You're funny," she said. "You're always just waiting and seeing."

She held out the bag, and Arlie took a chip.

"I wonder why she left West Virginia," Arlie said.

"She told me when Mrs. Rubio said I could show her to the bathroom. She said her dad likes moving. He says he won't be happy until he's lived in every state at least once."

"My grandpa lived everywhere except Alaska and Missouri," Arlie said. "And maybe Hawaii. I can't remember about Hawaii."

"Casey's moved a lot. Before West Virginia, she lived in Florida. Her dad owned a gas station, which she hated because his hands always smelled like motor oil. And she didn't like Florida very much. She said people always think that if you lived in Florida, you'd spend all day at the beach. But when you really live there, you hardly ever go. Which she didn't mind, because she hates the beach. Getting sand stuck to you. Sticky suntan lotion. I told her I *love* the beach, but she says it's dirty and hot." Belinda licked salt and crumbs off her thumb and shrugged. "Don't you think that would be hard? Moving all the time? How would you ever have any friends?"

Arlie nodded. She'd had a strange thought, listening to Belinda talk about Casey. She wanted to tell Belinda, but she couldn't. It was too weird. It would sound as though she'd lost her mind. What little was left of her mind, her mother would say.

"Casey says you get used to it, though," Belinda went on. "You make friends in a different way. Not the way you and I are friends. You know, almost like sisters. You don't get to know anyone like that."

Arlie kept nodding, trying to concentrate. This is crazy, she thought. This is completely nuts.

"She says you just pretend that going to school is like going to a party that you're only going to once. You'll meet a lot of kids and you might have fun with them, but you're never going to see them again, so why bother really getting to know them?"

Belinda reached into her bag and pinched the last chip between her thumb and forefinger. "Casey Lane. Lasey Cane. Hey, isn't that cool how it's a real name both ways?"

Arlie felt the world around her start to spin. She tried to say something, but nothing came out of her mouth.

"Arlie! What is it? What's the matter?"

She couldn't say a word.

"Are you choking? On a chip? If you're choking, point to your neck!" Belinda had taken first aid and CPR for a Girl Scout badge, and Arlie knew she was dying to do the Heimlich maneuver on someone real, not just a rubber dummy.

"I'm not choking!" Arlie managed to squeak.

Belinda looked as though she was about to burst into tears. Arlie couldn't tell if it was because she was so relieved

Arlie wasn't choking, or because she didn't actually get to do the Heimlich maneuver.

"Good Lord, Arlie!" she shrieked, sounding just like Mrs. Friedlander. "What's the matter with you, then?"

For a moment, Arlie thought she would be sick. The brilliant, sunny day was suddenly too bright; she wanted to hold her hand up against the glare.

"Lacey Caine," she said. "That's my mother's name."

four

All the way to Isabelle's, in the back of Mrs. Friedlander's Suburban, the girls said almost nothing. Mrs. Friedlander asked them about their day, and if they'd gotten their spelling tests back, and if Arlie had heard from her parents yet, and they answered as best they could. But Arlie's face was pale as milk, and her heart thumped wildly in her chest. Belinda knew enough not to ask her questions until they were alone.

At Isabelle's, Mrs. Friedlander gave permission for Belinda to spend the afternoon with Arlie. "I'll be back at five," she called as the girls headed for the apartment steps.

Not until they were in the lobby, waiting for the elevator, did Belinda whisper, "That's a pretty amazing coincidence."

"Wait," Arlie whispered back. "Just wait."

Upstairs, Arlie used her key. Isabelle wasn't home from work yet, and Michael was staying at Walter's until Isabelle could pick him up. Arlie shut the door and double-locked it, the way Isabelle had shown her. Finally, she turned and faced Belinda.

"It isn't just her name. It's a lot of things. Her father's a construction worker. So's my grandpa."

"Well, but—"

"And he used to own a gas station. My mom still talks

about how Grandpa's hands smelled. And how he'd wash and wash them, and they wouldn't get clean."

"That *is* kind of—"

"And remember when she said she didn't have a middle name? Well, my mother doesn't have one, either!"

They were standing in Isabelle's kitchen, which was really just a blue-tiled counter across from a sink, a stove, and a refrigerator. The counter was covered with ferns that Isabelle had watered that morning; there were puddles everywhere.

"Arlie," Belinda said, "what are you saying?"

"I don't know. I'm not saying anything. I just think it's weird, that's all."

"It's a coincidence. 'Weird' and 'coincidence' are two different things." Belinda looked nervous. "Hey. Where's that spider?"

"Tarantula. In the bedroom. Relax."

Belinda still looked nervous. "Can we have a snack?"

Arlie opened the refrigerator. "Sometimes she has strange stuff in here," she said, rummaging around. "Do you like yogurt?"

"No."

"How about raisins?"

"Just raisins?"

Arlie pulled her head out of the refrigerator. "Isabelle sprinkles them on celery covered with peanut butter."

"Ooh. That sounds good," Belinda said.

They made their snacks in silence. After they'd each taken their celery and some oatmeal cookies they found at the back of the refrigerator out to the living room, Arlie looked at Belinda. "Do you not want to talk about this?"

"It's not that," Belinda said. "It's just—what is there to talk about?"

"Well . . ." Arlie munched her celery, thinking. "We could see if Isabelle has any pictures of my mom around."

Belinda was quiet for a moment. "Okay," she finally said. "But only if you don't get too weird."

Belinda was afraid of the dark. She didn't like scary movies or dogs that jumped on her, and she only pretended to look forward to Halloween. She didn't even like firecrackers. "The way they pop makes me jump," she would say.

"You always like for everything to be . . ." Arlie couldn't think of the right word.

"What?" Belinda sounded almost angry. She never sounded angry.

Arlie felt her heart soften. "I won't get weird," she said. "But you have to admit. This is kind of exciting. And nothing exciting ever happens to us. We're always saying that."

Belinda nodded. "That's true."

"I just want to know more," Arlie said. "I can't pretend I don't know what I know."

"Yeah," Belinda said, "we can't."

Arlie smiled. "You're brave," she said.

"Not really. The opposite, actually."

"We're just going to look for a picture, that's all."

"And we're not going to snoop or look in drawers or in anything that's private." Belinda was nodding seriously.

"That's right. Only in places where Isabelle wouldn't mind." Arlie stood up and took both plates to the sink. "Come on. I know where she keeps her photo albums."

***

They pulled the albums off the bottom bookshelf in the living room.

"I love looking at pictures," Belinda said, almost happy again.

"Isabelle's had such a cool life. And she's only twenty-three. She's been in the Peace Corps, and helped build houses for poor people in Texas. One summer she worked at an animal sanctuary in Utah."

"What's a sanctuary?"

"A place where animals go if no one wants them, or if they were used for medical experiments, or in the circus. Isabelle says circuses are cruel."

"What did she do there?"

"Fed the animals and cleaned their stalls, mainly. Isabelle says abused animals need people to be around, so they can learn to feel safe again."

Again she felt it—that something big was going to happen. This time, though, the feeling made her stomach hurt.

Big in a bad way. That's how it felt this time.

"I'm going to do that when I get older," Belinda said. She opened the album on her lap. "Who are these people?"

Arlie looked over her shoulder. "College friends, I think," she said. The picture was of Isabelle and four friends standing in front of an old stone building with their arms around each others' shoulders. "She went to college in Pennsylvania. She said her favorite thing about college was eating doughnuts every morning in the old library before class."

"I'm going to that college," Belinda said, turning the page. "What's this?"

"Isabelle and her roommate riding in a hot-air balloon.

They gave rides to each other for a graduation present."

"If we go to the same college, don't give me that," Belinda said. "Just give me a sweater. Or money."

"This isn't the right book," Arlie said. "This is too new. We need stuff from when Isabelle was little."

"How far apart are they again?"

"Isabelle was born when my mom was fourteen."

"Wouldn't that be strange? Like having two moms," Belinda said. "My sisters are older, but at least they're still kids."

"Sometimes it's hard to believe Isabelle and my mom are even related," Arlie said, shutting the album and returning it to the bookshelf. She studied the remaining albums. "Maybe this one," she said, choosing the most tattered.

The pictures were older—you could tell by everyone's hair, and what they were wearing, and the cars in the background—and they were starting to fade. There were pictures of birthday parties and days at the beach: the kind of pictures where a grownup is trying to get kids to behave, but at the last minute the kids stick out their tongues and make goofy faces.

"Which one's Isabelle?" Belinda asked.

Arlie started to answer, then stopped.

"Is this her?" Belinda was pointing to a kid who might have been Isabelle—a laughing girl in a red bathing suit, holding a green plastic shovel.

When Arlie still didn't answer, Belinda looked at her. "What?" she asked, then followed Arlie's eyes to another picture on the page.

Arlie nodded at the picture. "Look," she said, not pointing. She didn't need to.

It was a picture of kids in front of a picnic table. Most of them were laughing and obviously jostling each other for position; one, a barefoot boy with a crew cut, was down on one knee, his arms spread, as if he were singing a showstopper and had just hit the last note. It was a picture of summer, a family reunion, a barbecue: you could almost smell steaks on a grill, suntan lotion, heat rising off the cement around a pool.

Only one child was off to the side, looking apart: a little stern, embarrassed by the fun around her. She wore a dress, and stood with her arms crossed on her chest.

"Oh, my God," Belinda breathed.

Bony elbows. Short brown hair, plain but neat, fastened with a clip. Small, abrupt nose. Watchful blue eyes.

"It's her," Arlie said.

Belinda's eyes were huge.

"My mom and her. Casey," Arlie said.

"You promised you wouldn't get weird," Belinda said.

"I'm not. I'm just saying. Who does this look like to you?"

"Lots of people have brown hair. And eyes like that. It doesn't mean anything."

"It's not the hair. Or the eyes. And you know it," Arlie said. Her stomach hurt like crazy.

"I admit, it does look an awful lot like her. An *awful* lot." Belinda leaned in close. "I still say it's a coincidence."

Arlie unstuck the photograph gently from the page and looked on the back. Someone had scrawled "Santa Cruz, 1977" in black ink. Before Isabelle was born. Mom would have been twelve, a year older than Arlie and Casey were now.

"A really *weird* coincidence," Belinda was saying.

Had her mother ever lived in Santa Cruz? Arlie tried to remember if Mom had ever said. What did she know about

Santa Cruz? That there was a university there and a beach and an amusement park.

Her mother had gone to college in Iowa. She hated beaches: too much sun gave you skin cancer, she said. Iowa was about as far away as you could get from a beach.

But this picture was taken when her mother was a girl, too young to decide on her own where she could live. She would have gone where Grandma and Grandpa had wanted to go. She wouldn't have had any say in the matter, something Arlie found almost impossible to imagine.

"Who are these other people?" Belinda was asking.

Arlie squinted and studied the photo. "I'm not sure," she said. "I think they're cousins. My mom has a lot of cousins." She pointed to the boy on his knee. "This one might be Clyde. He grew up on a farm."

"He looks like that," Belinda said. "Where is he now?"

"I think he's a nurse in Alabama."

"How come he isn't a doctor?"

Arlie shrugged. "I don't know. He just isn't."

Belinda sniffed and drew herself up straighter. "Boys aren't supposed to be nurses," she said.

Belinda could be like this. She didn't mean anything by it. She just liked for everything to be the way she expected it. Mostly Arlie ignored it.

"My mom's not close to her cousins anymore," Arlie said. "We never see them. I don't even know them."

"Anyway," Belinda said, fidgeting while Arlie studied the open album, "they're *your* relatives. Yours and your mom's and Isabelle's. Not Casey's. This doesn't prove anything."

"Except that Casey Lane looks almost exactly like my mom when she was a kid," Arlie said.

"Which still doesn't prove anything. Lots of people look alike. Once I heard my uncle say that my grandmother was the spitting image of Gregory Peck." Belinda looked back down at the album. "This picture is all faded and yellow anyway. You can't really tell anything."

Arlie was going to argue but decided not to. "Who's Gregory Peck?"

"Some actor. Really, Arlie, look. Your mom was taller than Casey. And there's something different about her hair. It's thicker or something."

"It's parted on the side."

"No, it's thicker. It's different hair. This is a different girl. This is your mother. A long time ago." Belinda sounded almost frantic. "Arlie. *Casey Lane is not your mother.*"

Arlie heard keys jingling in the front-door lock. A moment later, Isabelle and Michael came into the apartment. Michael dropped his backpack on the floor by the door and said, "Can I have a snack?" but Isabelle didn't answer him.

"What are you doing here?" Arlie asked. "I didn't think you got off work until later."

"Arlie. Michael. I need you to come sit with me," Isabelle said. Her face was white, her eyes squinty and red, as though she'd been rubbing them.

Arlie's stomach was suddenly killing her. "What is it? What's the matter?"

Isabelle didn't answer. Arlie and Michael followed her into the living room and sat down on the couch. Isabelle sat across from them on the low wooden coffee table. She didn't seem to even notice Belinda, who stood by the kitchen counter. Arlie could tell Belinda felt left out. It was scary how Isabelle hadn't smiled at her or even said hi. She'd met Belinda a hundred times before.

"Guys." Isabelle's voice was weird: formal and unfamiliar. "Your parents have been in a car accident. They've been taken to the hospital in Paso Robles in an ambulance."

Arlie couldn't feel her hands. "What?" she said. Her voice seemed to come from someone else's mouth.

Michael started to cry. "Are they dead?" he asked.

"No. They're hurt, though."

Arlie's scalp was tingling, and there was a buzzing in her head where the thinking was supposed to be. Across the room, Belinda had put both hands over her mouth.

"Pretty badly hurt," Isabelle said.

Why won't Michael stop screaming? Arlie thought, and then realized that the terrible sounds she was hearing were her own sobs.

"They're hurt," Isabelle said, "but they're alive."

five

The rest of the afternoon passed in a fog. Belinda left with her mother at five, giving Arlie a sad look and a quick hug. Michael finally stopped crying and announced loudly, "Mom and Dad got in a crash!" before absorbing himself in the task of stacking checkers pieces on top of each other and knocking them down with a butter knife. He did it over and over, until Isabelle, on the phone with the hospital, had to ask him to stop.

After Belinda went home, Arlie and Michael and Isabelle ate dinner. Isabelle made French toast and German potato salad, saying it was international and therefore educational, something Arlie and Michael's parents would approve of even though there were no vegetables involved. She mentioned their parents casually, as if nothing catastrophic had happened, and somehow Arlie understood that it was because of Michael, and not to ask questions until later.

After dinner, Michael took a bath. At first, he didn't want to use bubble bath, thinking it was just for girls, but Isabelle showed him some that came in a bottle shaped like an oil can. Arlie heard water running, and a minute later Isabelle emerged from the bathroom, closing the door behind her. Arlie's stomach, which had settled a little, knotted up again.

"What?" she asked, not really wanting to know.

Isabelle sighed and sank into a kitchen chair across from Arlie.

"The car crash. It was a bad one," she said. She met Arlie's gaze. "Your dad has cuts and bruises and a broken finger. And a machine to help him breathe, for now. They're checking for internal injuries."

A broken finger was bad for a drummer, Arlie thought. Mom was always saying that Dad had to be careful of his hands. She wouldn't let him take karate or fix things with a hammer. "It's your livelihood," she always said.

A broken finger was bad. That was what Isabelle meant by bad, maybe.

"Your mother," Isabelle said, and stopped.

Horrified, Arlie saw that her eyes were full of tears.

"Your mother is in a coma," Isabelle said. "We don't know how bad it is."

"What's a coma?" Arlie whispered, even though she was pretty sure she already knew.

"She's unconscious. She's not in any pain, though. It's like she's asleep."

"Unconscious is like dead."

"No, it's not." Isabelle reached across the table for Arlie's hand. "Listen. She's resting. Her body has been through a trauma. For now, she's stable."

"What's stable?" Arlie thought of horses stamping their hooves in their stalls, unable to turn around.

"She's okay. For now. We'll drive down to the hospital tomorrow. We'll find out more."

Arlie inhaled deeply. "She's not going to—"

Isabelle gripped her hand. "No," she said.

***

After his bath, Michael crawled into his sleeping bag and was snoring in an instant. Arlie still sat at the kitchen table, her math book open and unread in front of her. She watched as Isabelle rinsed the dinner dishes in the sink.

"How much older is Mom than you?" she asked.

"Fourteen years," Isabelle said. "You know that."

"Where was she born?"

"I don't know, sweetie. They moved around a lot."

"Even after you were born?"

Isabelle nodded. "Wanderlust is in Grandpa's blood."

Arlie swallowed. "What about Mom?"

"What about her?"

"Does she like to move?"

"Lacey?" Isabelle snorted. "She doesn't like to drive to the *post office*."

"This trip with Dad, then." Arlie bit her lower lip so she wouldn't cry. "Why did she even go?"

"She worries that he can't manage without her," Isabelle said. "She might be right," she added quietly.

"Manage what?"

"The hotels. The clubs. The directions. The paychecks. Since your father went bankrupt—" Isabelle paused as she scrubbed a plate under the running water. "You know your mom," she said finally.

"Not everything."

"No one knows everything about another person."

Arlie turned a page in her math book and pretended to study it. "Do you believe in magic?"

"Oh, bunny," Isabelle said. "Everything's going to be all right."

"I'm not talking about her getting better," Arlie said, still looking at the compound fractions on the page. "I'm talking about real magic."

"Well," Isabelle said, her mouth creasing downward as she considered, "yes. I do."

"Not like the magic of spring, or how magical it is when a baby is born, or even when you're thinking of a song and it suddenly starts playing on the radio. I mean real magic."

"Yeah, I do." Isabelle turned the faucet off and reached for a dish towel. "Come on. What?"

Around Belinda, Arlie had felt that her thoughts were silly and reckless. Now she felt careful, almost shy about what she wanted to say.

"I'm not sure about this," she began. "It's probably nothing. Just a weird coincidence. Probably."

"What? What?"

Arlie told. The low light from the reading lamp cast long shadows on the shelves, the worn purple rug, the gold curtains at the front window, Isabelle's face. On the street below, she could hear cars and, farther away, the low, slow rumble of the BART train as it pulled into the station, the hissing squeak of its doors opening to let passengers in and out. So many people. Sometimes, in a car on unfamiliar streets, Arlie would marvel at all the houses, each with its own family: people she didn't know, who didn't know her. Whose lives were utterly strange to her, but the same as hers, really—full of other people, and memories, and boring jobs that had to get done. And little things—laughing, feeling happy for no reason—that you didn't think about very often but that made you look forward to getting out of bed even when nothing exciting was supposed to happen. Big things, too, like vacations or getting an A, or having a baby, if you were a grownup.

As she finished telling her story to Isabelle, she wondered if she would ever feel like other people again. Other people's mothers weren't in comas.

"So what you're saying," Isabelle said slowly, her forehead wrinkling with concentration, "is that Casey Lane is your mom? Lacey?"

"That's not what I'm saying," Arlie said firmly.

Isabelle looked disappointed.

"Unless you think she *could* be," Arlie offered.

"Well, what do you think?"

"What I already said. That it's weird. And with Mom . . . sick—"

"I know," Isabelle said. "I was thinking the same thing."

There was a long pause. Outside, a car alarm blared suddenly.

"What are we thinking exactly?" Arlie finally asked.

Isabelle sighed. "Frankly, I don't know."

Great, Arlie thought. I shouldn't have told.

"Which is kind of what makes it magic, don't you think?" Isabelle asked.

"So what should I do?" Arlie asked.

Isabelle shrugged. "Just wait. See what happens. There's not a lot you *can* do, other than that."

Now it was Arlie's turn to be disappointed. "I hate not doing something," she said.

"I know," Isabelle said. "It's the hardest part."

After a minute, Arlie said, "I saw this show on TV once. About a lady inventor who got stuck in some space-time continuum thing. It was made up, but you were supposed to think it could really happen."

"Where'd you see this?"

"On TV. *Bart Blodgett Explains the Mysteries of the Universe*. A science show."

"What happened to the lady inventor?"

"She went back to Civil War days and told everyone about airplanes, but no one believed her. Bart Blodgett says the time has to be right for people to accept new ideas." Arlie stopped a moment, considering. "That's what I think, I guess."

Isabelle threaded the dish towel through the refrigerator door handle. "No time like the present, I always say."

"You don't always say that."

"Well," Isabelle said, turning back to face Arlie, "I'm saying it now."

The next morning, they headed out early, when the roads were almost empty. The sky, laced with streaky clouds, had just started to lighten. It reminded Arlie of other times she'd been awake and driving early in the morning. Mostly family car trips. Her dad liked to beat the rush-hour traffic.

They didn't talk much. For once, Isabelle didn't blast the radio. She set the dial to an oldies station and turned the volume down. The familiar songs were soothing, like lullabies. Arlie thought Michael had fallen asleep when, just south of Gilroy, he piped up.

"Ms. Guthrie'll be mad," he said.

"No, she won't. I called her, and Mrs. Rubio, too," Isabelle said. "They'll understand."

"You called them in the middle of the night?" he asked.

"I left a message at the school office. They have voice mail."

Michael was silent. Finally, he said, "Walter won't know where I am."

"Ms. Guthrie will tell him, I'll bet," Isabelle said.

More silence. "You're only supposed to miss school if you're sick," Michael said, but softly, almost to himself.

"It's all right, Michael," Isabelle said gently. "You get to miss it for emergencies, too."

Arlie looked out at the pretty pink sky, the ribbons of clouds, the distant hills studded with oak trees and grazing cows. On the radio, Cat Stevens—a musician her dad liked, whose name Arlie always thought was funny—sang "Peace Train," a song with a choir that sounded like music in a church.

Weird, to think this was an emergency.

They drove steadily, not stopping for anything except gas. Isabelle had brought apples and cheese for snacks, but Arlie wasn't hungry. She listened to the radio and slept a little, until they passed a road sign: PASO ROBLES 15 MILES.

"We're almost there," Isabelle said.

Michael shifted in his seat and opened his eyes. He didn't say a word.

"My stomach hurts," Arlie said.

"Maybe you're hungry," Isabelle said. "Have a piece of cheese."

"That's not it."

After a moment, Isabelle said, "You don't have to do anything you don't want to do, Arlie."

"You mean . . ." Pause. "See them?" she whispered.

"You can sit in the waiting room the whole time," Isabelle said.

"What do they look like?" Michael asked, as if they might be wearing costumes and funny masks and he wasn't sure he'd recognize them.

"Sometimes people in the hospital look different," Isabelle said. "A little scary."

"I'm not scared!" Michael said, but Arlie knew it was an act.

"You guys can hang out in the waiting room," Isabelle said. She flicked on her blinker and moved to the exit ramp. "I'll see what's what."

Arlie thought of her mother, the way she was always lecturing about people being assertive and standing up for themselves.

"Will Mom mind?" she asked.

"About what?"

"The waiting room." It seemed like a chicken thing to do, the kind of thing that would make Mom sigh in exasperation.

"Arlie," Isabelle said, looking in the rearview mirror and holding Arlie's gaze for an instant, "I'm not giving you a choice here. You and Michael are sitting in the waiting room. It's my decision."

Arlie nodded, thinking that she had never loved Isabelle more than she did at that moment.

It wasn't just Isabelle's decision. A nurse with a name tag reading JANICE made Arlie and Michael wait in the front lobby, which wasn't even on the same floor as the place where all the sick people were. No children in the ICU, she said firmly.

"Why do they call it that?" Michael asked, after Isabelle had left them with a stack of *Highlights* and a deck of old playing cards.

"It's not 'I See You.' It's not words. It's letters. I. C. U. It stands for something." Arlie had seen it on a sign by the hospital's front door.

Michael nodded, not really understanding, and looked around. "It's like an apartment building in here."

The only lobby he'd ever been in was at Isabelle's apartment building. "Come on. Let's play cards," Arlie said.

Michael's eyes lit up. "Go Fish!" he yelled.

"Shh! I'll play if you're quiet," she said.

As Arlie shuffled the cards, Michael said happily, "You hate Go Fish."

Arlie nodded and began to deal. She didn't admit that right now she didn't mind playing Go Fish; it was exactly what she felt like doing. Something easy and repetitive that she didn't have to think about.

"Fo Gish," she said, out of habit.

Trying to keep his pile of cards from falling off the slippery vinyl seat between them, Michael laughed. "Fo *Gish?*"

"It's Go Fish with the first letters reversed," she said. "Belinda and I do it all the time."

Michael laughed again. It occurred to Arlie that he was only two years older than Jesse Sweeney but a lot more fun.

"Try it," she said.

His face wrinkled in concentration. "Fold gish," he said carefully, trying to get it right.

"Goldfish. Good. Only it doesn't always have to be 'fish,'" Arlie said. "You can do it with other words."

Michael looked around. "Raiting Woom," he said.

"Hey! Good!"

"Larking pot!" he said, pointing.

Arlie laughed a little too loudly, and Michael held his finger to his lips. "Shh! You said," he whispered.

"Okay, okay." Now it was her turn to think of one. "Gecurity Sard," she said, pointing to the man in uniform standing near the elevator.

"Security guard! This is fun!"

It was. They went back and forth, Go Fish forgotten, until Michael blurted out, "Car crash!" Instantly, Arlie's blood seemed to freeze solid.

"That doesn't work," she said. "It's the same letter at the beginning of each word."

Michael, looking shocked at himself, nodded solemnly.

"Come on," Arlie said quietly. "Let's play cards."

They took up the cards and busied themselves trying to put them in order. Arlie blinked back tears. She knew it wasn't fair, that she was being mean, but she couldn't help it. At that moment, she hated Michael. Because he had reminded her. Because he was too little to understand. Because she had to take care of him, when all she wanted was for someone to take care of her.

They played for a half hour, until Arlie was so bored she could barely keep her eyes open. Then they read magazines. Arlie was on her last *Highlights* and wondering what she was going to do next when she saw Isabelle emerge from the elevator across the room. Michael ran to her and threw his arms around her hips, but Arlie stayed where she was, waiting for Isabelle to come to her. As she approached, Arlie saw that her eyes were red.

"How are you guys doing?" she asked, tousling Arlie's hair.

"I won Go Fish forty-eight times!" Michael said.

"We're okay," Arlie said. Waiting.

But all Isabelle said was "Come on. Let's go."

Michael looked up from where he had wound himself around Isabelle's legs. "What about Mom and Dad?" he asked.

"They're fine," Isabelle said, in a way that Arlie knew meant they weren't. "They're resting."

"Can't we see them?" Michael asked. Without waiting for an answer he started to cry. "I want to see them."

"Not this time, sweetheart," Isabelle said, pulling Michael's arms off her and kneeling down to hug him.

Arlie watched as Michael buried his face in her neck. "I *want* to," he sobbed over and over as Isabelle patted his back, ignoring the other people in the room, who were pretending not to notice them.

Arlie briefly considered approaching them—it would be nice to be hugged. But she hung back, embarrassed by everyone watching. And also not wanting Isabelle to think she was jealous of Michael getting all the attention.

The drive home took longer than the drive there: traffic was heavier, and there was an accident in Fremont that slowed them down even more. Arlie closed her eyes as they crawled past the dented cars on the side of the road. Darn rubber-neckers, she heard her dad say in her head.

Isabelle didn't say a word until they were almost home and Michael had dozed off a second time. Then she looked back at Arlie in the rearview mirror.

"They're the same," she said. "No change."

Arlie looked out the window, too tired even to nod.

"It's going to be that way for a while," Isabelle said.

More waiting. What she hated most.

"I'm sorry, bunny."

It's not *your* fault, Arlie thought. It's nobody's fault.

Then she wondered, Who do you get mad at when it's nobody's fault?

The next morning before the bell rang, Belinda hovered near Arlie, not touching her exactly but staying close. "How's your mom?" she asked when no one else was around.

"In a coma. It's when—"

Belinda laid a hand on Arlie's shoulder. Like a grownup. A mom, even. "I know what it is," she said.

Arlie wanted to act like Jesse did when he stubbed his toe. She wanted to sob, to screech, to rest her head on Belinda's shoulder and let herself be hugged and patted.

Instead, she said, "She's fine. Isabelle says she's just resting."

Belinda nodded, knowing, without being told, that it was a secret, just between them.

When Arlie entered the classroom, Mrs. Rubio called her up to the front desk.

"Dear," she said, "How are you doing?"

"Fine," Arlie said automatically. As much as she liked Mrs. Rubio, she didn't like a teacher calling her "dear."

"You let me know if you need anything," Mrs. Rubio said. "Anything at all. Do as much of your homework as you can manage. Don't worry if you can't finish some nights."

"I can finish," Arlie said. She always did her homework. Not doing it would mean not being herself, and she was already having trouble remembering who she was, who she had been—a normal kid—the day before.

"All right, then," Mrs. Rubio said when Arlie had taken her seat. "Who's ready for auditions?"

It was the nicest thing she could have done. Like medicine, Arlie thought, or pulling up the shades on a dreary day.

She sat up straight. She was Arlie Metcalfe, who was good in school and did her homework and was going to try out for the class play. Her parents were away on a trip. They would be back in four weeks.

Everything was okay.

The kids had all begun talking at once. Except Casey, Arlie noticed, turning around in her chair. She's too new, Arlie thought. She doesn't have anyone to talk to yet.

Mrs. Rubio stood at each desk group and asked everyone which part he or she wanted to try out for. Then she thumbed through her pile of scripts and pulled out the right one.

Belinda nudged her. "Who do you want to be?"

Arlie said, "I still don't know." And it was true: she didn't. She'd been so busy thinking about Casey Lane, and *not* thinking about her parents, that she hadn't given it much attention. Now she was annoyed with herself: she wished she'd been concentrating on the play, something she cared about, something that was part of real life.

"Well, I'm going to try out for the grandmother," Belinda said. "She gets to wear a shawl."

"Hmm," Arlie said, studying the list of characters Mrs. Rubio had displayed on the overhead projector.

Just then she became aware of Mrs. Rubio at Casey's desk group. "How about you, Casey?" Mrs. Rubio was saying. "Anything grabbing you?"

"I want to be Charlie," Casey said.

Charlie was a very small part. Arlie was surprised. Casey seemed like the kind of girl who would want a big part.

"Good for you," Mrs. Rubio said, pulling a script marked "Charlie" out of her pile. "No reason a girl can't try out for a male character."

Casey smiled a little. "That's why they call it acting," she said.

Arlie felt the blood in her veins begin to race. Hey, that's what *Isabelle* said, she thought. That's what *I* said.

Mrs. Rubio beamed. "Why, that's right!" she said.

Arlie's insides churned. "Petey," she said to no one in particular, crossing her arms over her chest. "I'm trying out for Petey."

"Hey," Warren said, overhearing her. "I'm trying out for Petey, too."

Arlie shot him a look. "The more the merrier," she said icily.

Jeremy snorted. "You idiot. You freak," he said. "You can't try out for a boy's part."

"Watch me," Arlie said. Then she added, "At least I can read all the lines."

Jeremy turned away and made a big show of trying to throw an eraser into the wastebasket at Mrs. Rubio's desk. He was flushed, though: Arlie knew she'd hurt his feelings. Jeremy wasn't a very good reader.

For a moment, she didn't even recognize herself.

Mrs. Rubio stood before her. "Okay, gang," she said. "Who wants what?"

Belinda said, "The grandmother, please." Jeremy, seeming not to care, said, "Town folk, I guess." Warren and Arlie asked for Petey's script.

This time, Arlie noticed, when Mrs. Rubio handed her the script, she didn't say "Good for you" or anything at all. She was already used to the idea of a girl trying out for a boy's part, so Arlie's doing it was no big deal.

"That's a lot of words," Belinda said, leaning over to read.

"You big ole freak," Jeremy whispered across the table.

"Hey," Warren said. "Why don't you shut up for a change?"

Arlie gave him a grateful look. "Good luck on Petey," she said, deciding that she wouldn't even really mind losing out to Warren.

"You, too," Warren said.

"It was weird, her saying that thing about why they call it acting," Belinda said at recess.

"And she said a boy should try out for a boy character. She *said* that." Xenia flicked her long braid over her shoulder.

"Maybe she just changed her mind," Arlie said.

"She sounded pretty sure of herself," Belinda said.

Arlie had already decided that Casey might be the kind of girl who said one thing and did another. The kind of girl you couldn't really trust. But somehow, she didn't want everyone else to think that, too.

"And saying 'That's why they call it acting' makes her sound like she's such a *grownup*," Xenia said. "Like she's so *worldly*. Like she even knows who 'they' are."

Belinda nodded. "Eleven-year-olds don't know why anybody calls it acting."

"Hey," Xenia said with a nod. "Look who's coming over."

Casey was heading toward them, her eyes not exactly smiling but not looking down or away, either. The curly ends of her hair bobbed slightly.

Watching her, Arlie remembered everything that she hadn't been thinking about all morning: her mom and dad lying in a hospital, Mom not awake even though it was already lunchtime. Her stomach clenched like a fist.

"Hi," Casey said. She sat neatly on their bench, off to one end, making sure to tuck her skirt under her thighs.

"Where were you?" Belinda asked.

"I had to talk to the principal," Casey said. "Stuff about my old school."

"How come you always wear dresses?" Arlie asked.

Casey's left hand smoothed her skirt over her leg. "I just like them."

"No one else wears them," Xenia said.

Casey shrugged. "I don't care."

Arlie felt a grudging respect. "Hey," she said, "I thought you said boys should try out for boy characters' parts."

"I said *maybe*."

That might be true, Arlie thought. "How come you didn't try out for Petey, then?"

"I never know how long I'm going to be somewhere," Casey said. "I figured if I have to move before the play gets performed, it isn't fair to have a big part."

"That makes sense, I guess," Belinda said.

Arlie felt bad, the way she always did when Belinda was nicer than she was. But she was relieved, too: she didn't want her friends to dislike Casey.

Then she felt a shiver of worry. What would it mean if Casey left?

"Who are you going to try out for?" Casey asked Arlie.

It was a little embarrassing, the way she only asked Arlie, as if Belinda and Xenia weren't even there.

"Petey," Arlie said.

"Oh." Casey sounded surprised. "'Cause you said the other day you were trying out for the grandmother."

I did? Arlie thought.

As if she could read Arlie's thoughts, Belinda nodded. "Yeah, you did. You said it was the best girl part."

"Oh, yeah," Arlie said. She fidgeted, as though she'd been the one who'd tried to fool everyone. "I changed my mind," she said.

After a minute, Casey said, "You just have to practice."

Did she mean Arlie needed more practice than anyone else? They looked at each other. Something passed between them—not hate, really, or anger, or anything Arlie had ever felt before. Something harder to pin down. A glint of understanding.

An I-know-exactly-who-you-are kind of understanding.

Which was funny, Arlie thought, because the more she thought she knew exactly who Casey was, the less she understood anything at all.

Six

Walking to Room 22 after lunch, Casey hung back with Arlie. "You want to come over after school?" she asked. "I could help you memorize your lines."

"What about *your* lines?" Arlie asked.

"I don't need help," Casey said.

Arlie felt her heart harden.

"I don't have that many," Casey said.

"Well," Arlie said. She didn't like being the only one who needed help; still, it was tempting to have somewhere new to go, something other than her parents to think about.

"I have to check with my aunt," she said.

"Neat," Casey said.

They walked together in silence.

"We could ask Belinda and Xenia," Arlie said, keeping her voice low since they were right behind her.

"It's hard to work with four people," Casey said. "Let's do it with just us."

At the door to Room 22, Casey whispered, "Ask Mrs. Rubio if you can call your aunt on the classroom phone."

As if they were best friends.

"She says we can't use that phone for personal calls," Arlie said.

"Leave it to me," Casey said.

Arlie didn't like leaving things to other people. She didn't like Casey's trying to run things.

"I'm really good at getting teachers to make exceptions," Casey said.

Casey went right up to Mrs. Rubio. Arlie couldn't hear a word she said, but there was a lot of nodding.

When the three o'clock bell finally rang, Mrs. Rubio called Arlie up to her desk.

"Casey tells me that she has her heart set on having you over this afternoon, Arlie," she said quietly. "I think it's lovely that you're making her feel welcome. And it will be nice for you, too. . . ."

Her voice trailed off. Arlie hated how someone's being in a coma made everyone else nervous. Even grownups like Mrs. Rubio, who rode motorcycles and went scuba diving.

"She says you forgot your note this morning," Mrs. Rubio went on.

"I—"

"I'm going to make an exception. If you'd like to call your aunt from my phone, you may do so," Mrs. Rubio said.

"But I—"

"You know the rules about bringing a note. But *just this once* . . ." Mrs. Rubio shook her finger at Arlie. "I've got an appointment, though, so make it quick."

"Go. It'll be nice for you," Isabelle said when Arlie reached her at the wildlife museum.

"Have you heard anything?" Arlie asked quietly.

"I talked to the doctor this morning," Isabelle said. "Your dad's doing much better. Your mom's—"

"It's okay," Arlie said. "You don't have to tell me."

"I'm not trying to keep anything from you, bunny," Isabelle said. "There's just nothing to tell. Your mom is stable. Still in a coma. But she's okay."

How can you be in a coma and be okay at the same time? Arlie thought.

"The doctor says this happens. She's resting. Her body is resting. And we won't really know anything for a while."

Suddenly, there were a million things Arlie wanted to ask. Not with Mrs. Rubio right behind her, though.

"Go to Casey's. I'll pick you up around five-thirty," Isabelle was saying. "Have a good time."

Impossible, Arlie thought. But she hung up the phone, thanked Mrs. Rubio, and went out into the hall. "I can go," she said to Casey.

Within minutes, they were heading down Magnolia Avenue.

"I like this house almost more than any other I've ever lived in," Casey said. "Not as much as the one in Pennsylvania, because that one was near a duck pond. But this one's pretty nice. There's a fireplace."

She didn't say it as if she was bragging, but Arlie was still mad about her making Mrs. Rubio think she'd forgotten to bring a note, like some kindergartner.

"My mom says there are kids in the neighborhood about my age, but that never works out," Casey said.

"Why not?"

"They already have their own friends," Casey said simply. "It's too hard to break in."

They walked a bit in silence. The houses were newer than the ones in Arlie's neighborhood, and they all looked the same. There weren't many cars parked along the sidewalk, and there weren't any bikes or basketball hoops or swing sets in anybody's yard. Quiet and tidy, Arlie decided, in a lonely sort of way. It didn't look as though anyone really lived there.

Casey's house was yellow-brown with white trim, just like the houses on either side of it. Arlie could tell that one of the front windows belonged to a bedroom because of the white filmy curtains.

"Is your mom home?" she asked.

Casey shook her head. "She works."

"What does she do again?"

"She's a secretary."

Hmm, Arlie thought. Lots of people were secretaries. Was Grandma Ellen ever one? She would have to ask Isabelle.

"She just started yesterday, so she told me she'd be staying late," Casey said, fumbling in her pocket for her key. "To make a good impression."

"What does she look like?" Arlie asked.

Casey gave her a strange look. "My mom?" She turned and put the key in the lock. "I don't know. Like a mom."

"Well, but what color hair does she have? What color eyes?" Arlie knew she sounded weird, but she couldn't stop. "Is she tall? Is she thin?"

"Like me, I guess."

"Do you have a picture of her?"

Casey pushed at the front door. "Somewhere."

As soon as they entered the front hall, Arlie understood. Everything was still in boxes. She could see them piled high in the living room to the right, the dining room to the left. Boxes everywhere: on the darkly polished floor, the light blue sofa, the massive dining room table with a single leg, like a pedestal.

"What's in all these?" she asked.

"Everything," Casey said.

Arlie looked around. It seemed like so much stuff. Would everything she and her family owned fit in this many boxes? She hadn't ever thought about it.

"I've never moved before," she said.

"You get used to it," Casey said. She set her books on the floor beneath a table stacked high with boxes. It suddenly occurred to Arlie that Casey didn't have a backpack.

"You want a snack?" Casey asked.

They made their way through the dining room, along a path between boxes marked "Plates" and "Fragile—Glass-ware." Whose handwriting? Arlie tried to remember Grandma's and Grandpa's signatures on birthday cards. Nothing looked familiar. She couldn't wait to get a look at Casey's room.

They went into the kitchen and each loaded a plate with two chocolate chip cookies, three strawberries, and a lemon bar. Arlie didn't like anything with lemon in it, but Casey insisted, saying, "You should try *this* one, though." Then they climbed the stairs and entered Casey's room at the end of the hall. It, too, was full of boxes. Arlie looked around. Except for the neatly made twin bed, the desk with its organized array of paper and pens, and a straight-backed chair, everything was in boxes.

Arlie lowered herself to the floor. "What's in all these?"

Casey took a delicate bite of lemon bar. "Sometimes I almost forget," she said. "I keep everything in boxes until I'm sure we'll be staying for at least a little while."

"That must be hard," Arlie said. "I'd miss my stuff."

The bed had plain white sheets and a flowery spread.

The hem of the top sheet was folded over the spread, just the way Arlie's mom made her bed at home. Just the way Arlie and Michael were taught to make theirs. Every morning. No matter what. "Who cares?" Arlie would say, and Mom would answer, "*I* care, and so should you."

"Do you collect stuff?" Arlie asked.

"My mom says not to," Casey said, chewing and swallowing. "She says things that don't have a purpose are dust catchers."

"Hey!" Arlie said. "My mom says that all the time."

They laughed.

For a moment, it didn't matter whether Casey Lane was who she said she was, or some impossible incarnation of her mother, or someone else entirely. At that moment, she was just a friend. Arlie forgot about being bossed into trying a lemon bar.

"Fish," Casey said. "I collect fish."

Arlie stopped chewing.

"Glass fish, right?" she said.

"Yeah," Casey said. "They're all packed up. In bubble wrap and newspaper. How did you know?" She gave Arlie a squinty look. "You don't collect them, do you? Because that would be a strange coincidence."

"Oh, yeah," Arlie said. "*That* would be strange, all right." She made herself take another bite of her cookie in an effort to look casual. "My mom collects them," she said.

"I try to buy one from each state we've lived in," Casey said. "Maybe someday I'll have one from all fifty."

"Do you know what box they're in?" Arlie said. "Can I see them?"

"They're pretty special," Casey said uncertainly. "I don't

take them out when there are other people around. They might get broken."

"I won't break them. I won't even *touch* them. I just want to *see* them."

"Maybe another time," Casey said, just like a grownup. Just like a mom.

Arlie felt a wave of sadness. She remembered her mother watching Michael eat his Brussels sprouts the other night at dinner. Arlie had wanted to say "I *will* miss you"; had even thought about saying "Don't go." Would her parents have reconsidered their plans if she had? Maybe not—probably not—but now she would never know. And it felt as though she should have done something; that if she *had* done something, her mother would be home, in the little house with yellow paint and the tidy patch of grass. reminding her about homework and babysitting and overdue library books and dust bunnies under the bed.

Maybe there was more she could do now. Suddenly, it seemed as though the improbable, inexplicable fact of Casey Lane existed for a reason. Maybe it was a puzzle of some sort, and it was up to Arlie to solve it, to figure out how to put the pieces together in just the right way, so that her mom would be okay. A test, except that she didn't know who was giving it or what any of the right answers were. But maybe if she passed it, everything would be all right.

"What's your favorite movie?" she asked Casey.

"*Gone with the Wind*. Why?"

"What are your hobbies?"

Casey thought. "It's hard to have hobbies when you move around so much. Does packing count?"

"No. Something you like to do for fun."

"Reading, I guess. Why are you asking me all this?"

"Just to get to know you."

"Well . . ." Casey hesitated. "It's the way you're asking me. Like you already know what I'm going to say before I say it."

"Sorry." Arlie tried to take a breath, slow herself down. "Just one more thing."

"What?" Casey checked her watch, as if she suddenly wanted Arlie to go home. "We don't have much time."

"What's your favorite book?" Arlie asked.

Her eyes were on the square of late-afternoon light falling on the dusty floorboards, warm and golden, the perfect place for a cat to curl up, if Casey had a cat, which Arlie knew she didn't. Because she knew, without having to ask, that Casey would think cats were messy, and smelled.

"Oh, that's easy," Casey said, her eyes lighting up. *"Hans Brinker and the Silver Skates."*

Arlie smiled, not afraid the way she'd thought she might be, not even very surprised.

"It's a really good book," Casey said. "You should read it."

"Any news?" Arlie asked Isabelle after dinner that night. Michael was in Isabelle's room listening to the radio.

Isabelle shook her head. "What about you?" she asked. "Did you have fun at the new girl's?"

"It was okay." Arlie didn't look up from what she was working on at the kitchen table.

Isabelle scooched into the chair across from Arlie. "Just okay? What did you do over there?"

"Ate a lemon bar."

"That's not what I mean."

"It wasn't bad."

"*Arlie Ellen Metcalfe.*" Isabelle sounded as close to being a grownup as it was possible for her to sound. "What are you doing?"

"Making a list."

"What list?"

Arlie put her pen down and picked up the paper. "All the weird things about Casey and Mom," she said. "So far I've got ten."

Isabelle sipped tea from a fat green mug that said SAVE THE CALIFORNIA BANANA SLUG. "Like what?"

"Like she has no middle name. Like her dad is a construction worker and used to own a gas station and likes to move around. And how Casey Lane and Lacey Caine are almost the same. And how she says 'neat' all the time, and wears old-fashioned dresses."

"Hmm."

"Her favorite movie is *Gone with the Wind*. Her favorite book is *Hans Brinker.*"

"Amazing."

"You should meet her," Arlie said. "Do you want to? Maybe I can have her over on a Saturday, when you'd be around."

"Well, maybe. But—"

"But what?"

Isabelle smiled. "Casey Lane is happening to *you,* bunny. She's your mystery. Maybe it would be better if I didn't meet her just yet."

Arlie nodded. Part of her didn't have any idea what Isabelle meant; part of her understood perfectly. After a moment, she said, "She collects glass fish."

Isabelle set her tea down on the scarred wood table. "Really?"

Arlie nodded. "They're all in boxes, so I couldn't see them. But she told me."

"Too bad you couldn't get a look at any of them. Because your mom's fish are very distinctive."

"What do you mean?"

"She always scraped her initials on the base of each figure. On the underside, so you couldn't see them." She smiled and shook her head. "I always wanted one of those fish."

"Why didn't *you* collect them?"

"I collected owls. And I always wanted to trade her an owl for a fish. Just one. Fair and square. But she wouldn't. 'They're too important to me,' she used to say." She raised the tea to her lips and sipped. "She wouldn't part with a single one."

Michael thumped into the room. "Hey, Isabelle, do you want to lose weight?"

"No," she said. "Why?"

"Because banging your head against the wall burns a hundred and fifty calories an hour," Michael said.

"Where did you hear that?" Isabelle asked.

"On the radio," he answered. "They just said."

"Good to know," Isabelle said. "I'll keep it in mind."

After Michael had run back to Isabelle's room, Arlie whispered, "Doesn't he get it?"

"Get what?"

"That they're hurt. That Mom is . . ."

Isabelle shook her head. "He's only six, bunny. He doesn't understand the way you do."

I don't understand anything, Arlie thought.

"Don't let him fool you," Isabelle said. "He's pretty upset."

Briefly, Arlie thought of him standing in the driveway, forehead to forehead with Mom. At least he knows she loves him, she thought bitterly. I don't know anything.

She sighed. "It almost doesn't matter whether Casey carves her initials on her fish. Or has a middle name. Or anything."

When Isabelle didn't answer, Arlie said, "It's something else. Something weird. I can't explain it."

"What?" Isabelle asked softly.

The kitchen light spilled over the table and chairs like sunlight filtering through trees, warmth for just them. Beyond the table, the living room was dark, a shadowy presence, its furniture and books just shapes, barely visible.

"It's how Casey makes me feel," Arlie said. "Like I'm not good enough. Like I need to do better."

When she couldn't go on, Isabelle reached out and covered Arlie's hand with hers. "I know," she said.

Arlie swallowed. "Like today. She listened to me read my lines. She said I sounded like a girl pretending to be a boy. And I said, 'So?' Because I *am* a girl. Right?"

"Well," Isabelle said. "She has a point."

"What?" Arlie was outraged. Isabelle was always on her side.

"Maybe she just meant you had to do a little more than read the lines," Isabelle said.

"I *did* do more," Arlie said. "I read with *feeling*."

"That's good."

"But Casey kept saying to make my voice lower. And to stand kind of hunched over, like this." Arlie stood up, tucked her hands in her front pockets, and stuck her head forward.

"That looks like most of the guys I know," Isabelle said. "How'd she do?"

"She barely read her lines at all. She said she works better alone." Arlie sighed. "I'd memorized all my lines by the time you picked me up, but it was like she didn't even notice. She didn't care. She just kept telling me everything I wasn't doing right."

Again Arlie was close to tears.

There was a thumping sound from the bedroom.

"Michael!" Isabelle called. The thumping stopped. "You don't need to lose any weight!"

Arlie sniffed hard. "Anyway," she said, testing her voice.

Isabelle turned back to her.

"Listen, sweetheart," she said. "I can't explain any of this. It's weird, all right. But I can't explain how birds know where to fly when it starts to get cold, either."

Arlie nodded.

Isabelle reached across the table. "The way I see it, you've been given an incredible gift," she said. "And you're spending an awful lot of time trying to figure out how you got it."

From the bedroom came the unmistakable sound of yodeling.

"Maybe," Isabelle said, her voice almost a whisper, "you should just unwrap it."

seven

Mrs. Rubio called for quiet first thing the next morning, and everyone immediately stopped talking. Under their desks, Belinda nudged Arlie with her knee. "I hope we do it now," she whispered.

Arlie nodded in agreement. She was afraid that if Mrs. Rubio made them wait, all the words she'd memorized would just fly out of her head.

"Okay, guys," Mrs. Rubio said. "Let's start with Petey's friends."

It was just like Mrs. Rubio to start with the smaller parts first. Arlie knew she didn't want people to think Petey was going to get any special treatment.

Curtis Little, Robert Stuckey, and Casey were trying out for Charlie. Blake Barclay, Trevor Lisle, and Eduardo Vega were trying out for Sam. "It has to be Sam, though," Eduardo said. "If I don't get Sam, don't put me down for Charlie."

"How come?" Warren called out from his seat.

"I don't want to be anyone named Charlie," Eduardo said. "My cousin's name is Charlie. He picks his nose with his tongue."

"Eduardo, please!" Mrs. Rubio said.

"Anyway," Eduardo said. "I'd rather be a town folk."

"I guess I understand," Mrs. Rubio said. "Curtis, let's start with you."

Arlie had thought it would be fun listening to everybody try out. Actually, it was boring. The boys stumbled over their lines and giggled in embarrassment when Mrs. Rubio tried to cue them. Just like boys not to take it seriously, Arlie thought, and then noticed that Warren was practicing at his seat, checking the script in his lap, then closing his eyes and mouthing his lines silently. Arlie suddenly liked him even more than usual. Or maybe she just admired the way he didn't care what anybody thought, didn't seem to mind not fitting in.

After Mrs. Rubio had lectured the boys about taking pride in their work, she auditioned innkeepers, washer-people, and shoemakers. Some people knew their lines well; others faltered, giggled, stared at the floor, shifted from one foot to the other, blushed. Angela Bordman kept making Mrs. Rubio go back to the beginning, even though the innkeeper only had three lines.

When Mrs. Rubio said, "Let's do Petey," Arlie and War-ren rose and went to stand by the blackboard. Looking out over the sea of her classmates, Arlie caught sight of Casey, who didn't smile. She mouthed, *Go slow,* and nodded seri-ously. Arlie looked away. Her heart was in her throat. She should have brought a prop—a hat, maybe, to make her look more like a farmer. It would have been just the thing to sway Mrs. Rubio. Now she felt as though all her memorizing wouldn't even matter. And she'd spent two hours in front of Isabelle's full-length mirror the night before, practicing standing like a boy. All for nothing.

The scene they'd had to memorize was the one in which Petey's grandparents told him how much work there was to do that weekend: load the strawberries and cantaloupes and snap beans and peaches into the truck, drive to the fruit stand, get rid of the old crates and bins, arrange the new ones, discard any rotting fruit, sweep the floors, greet the customers.

"Working at a fruit stand sucks," Warren whispered to Arlie.

"Warren?" Mrs. Rubio settled herself at her desk with a clipboard and a pencil. "Why don't we start with you?"

Warren remembered all his lines, but he read them in a booming, too-low voice, as though he were on one side of a busy freeway and the audience was on the other.

"Warren?" Mrs. Rubio interrupted, gently pushing the air in front of her down with her hand.

"I'm just thinking about everyone at Leisure Valley," Warren said. "A lot of them have hearing aids."

"They could be *dead* and still hear you," Jeremy said.

"Just tone it down a little," Mrs. Rubio said.

Warren nodded, but when he went back to reading, he sounded the same. Every now and then, he took a step forward and raised his fist, as though he were giving a speech or volunteering to die for a good cause. To Arlie, he didn't look like someone who was supposed to be throwing away rotting peaches.

"Now you, Arlie," Mrs. Rubio said, after Warren had made a stiff little bow to the class.

Arlie smiled, sure that she was ready and happy to be following Warren. Mean as it was, she thought he was probably out of the running.

Then it happened. Her heart began to pound—hard. She thought that if she looked down, she might see it pound inside her sweater. Her hands shook, and her knees felt rubbery, as though they were too weak to hold up her body. For a minute she thought she might be sick. What would she do if she threw up right there, in front of Mrs. Rubio and everybody? Alex Manfredi had thrown up in kindergarten, but he'd had colitis, and besides, kindergartners were always throwing up. Not fifth graders. Not Arlie.

She got through her reading. Just barely. She couldn't hear her own thoughts, let alone the words that were coming out of her mouth. She didn't think she missed any lines, although she couldn't be sure. Her heart hurt. She thought maybe the whole class could hear the blood thumping in her veins.

The class clapped politely, and she fought the urge to hunch her shoulders and rush to her seat. She stood up straight—the way Casey had reminded her to—and forced herself to look out at the room and all the clapping kids. It was a blur, like putting her head underwater and trying to see something lying at the bottom of the pool.

"Thank you, Arlie," Mrs. Rubio said.

When she got back to her seat, Belinda whispered, "Great job."

"Did I look weird?" Arlie whispered back. "Did I say all the right words?"

For some reason, she thought of Mr. Cunningham saying that he knew what he really looked like, even without a mirror. Arlie had no idea what she looked like. It was as though someone else—a stranger—had just auditioned, forcing Arlie out of her own body to do it.

"Yeah," Belinda said. "You said everything right."

"I mean—" Arlie paused. "Was I all red? Could you hear me breathing?"

"What are you talking about?" Belinda turned her attention to the kids lining up for the shoemaker. "You were fine."

Arlie forced herself to relax, thinking that the gulf between what Belinda said and how she had actually felt was unbridgeable. It was as if she didn't know how people saw her, or who she really was.

"I've been thinking," Arlie said at lunch, "that I don't even want to be Petey."

Belinda and Xenia were at the water fountain. Arlie didn't know why she was telling Casey this.

"You should talk louder," Casey said. "And slowly. You were rushing."

"I was so scared," Arlie said. "I felt like I was falling, or being chased. I couldn't breathe."

"And you forgot to shove your hands in your pockets," Casey said. "Boys always shove their hands in their pockets."

So far, she hadn't said one nice thing.

"Maybe I don't really want to do this," Arlie said, even though she was pretty sure that the reason she was so nervous was because she did want to do it. A lot.

"You'll get it," Casey said matter-of-factly. "That Warren kid was terrible."

Arlie sipped her fruit punch and eyed Casey with irritation. Belinda had said three times how good she was. Arlie didn't really believe her, but it was nice to hear just the same. Then she realized that she hadn't said anything nice about Casey's tryout, either.

"You were good," she said, trying to make amends.

Casey smiled and shrugged, as though it didn't really matter if she had been good or not. "Try to remember about your hands next time," she said. "And being loud."

Arlie saw Belinda and Xenia bounding toward them. "Don't say anything," Arlie whispered.

She didn't want Belinda to know how scared she had felt. With Belinda, Arlie was always the brave one.

Casey nodded, as though she was used to being the keeper of other people's secrets, and Arlie thought that even though she didn't like Casey in some ways, she knew the new girl wouldn't tell.

Mrs. Rubio announced the parts the next morning. When she said, "Arlie Metcalfe will play the role of Petey," Arlie felt like vomiting into her desk.

Belinda was Grandma, and Warren was Grandpa. Xenia was the shoemaker, and, not surprisingly, Jeremy Sanchez was a town folk. Casey was Charlie, and Eduardo Vega was happy to be Sam. "Yes!" he said when Mrs. Rubio called his name.

Curtis Little looked at him. "Hey, how does your cousin do that thing with his tongue?"

"Anyone who misbehaves at any time during the rehearsals or the performances of this play will be replaced immediately," Mrs. Rubio said. Everyone got very quiet. "No one is irreplaceable."

Was this true? Mrs. Rubio said it a lot when she was trying to get the class to realize that privileges could be as easily taken away as given. Usually, Arlie just accepted it as fact. Today, though, it struck her as untrue, something Mrs. Rubio was just saying to get everyone to behave.

Casey raised her hand. "You said 'performances,'" she said. "I thought there was just one."

"I'm a stickler for accuracy," Arlie's mom was always

saying. Arlie winced: she felt a little stabbing under one rib.

"We're going to do one performance for Leisure Valley and another for the parents. They might like to see what all the fuss is about," Mrs. Rubio said.

"Can grandmothers come?" Warren asked.

"Of course," Mrs. Rubio said. "Everyone is welcome."

"I'm not sure about my uncle," Warren said. "He's a pilot. He might be flying somewhere."

"Don't worry, Warren. It will all work out," Mrs. Rubio said.

Arlie pretended to look for clean paper. Riffling through her notebook, she bit her lip to keep from crying. It was bad enough that she'd gotten the part. To have to play it to a roomful of parents, minus her own, was almost more than she could bear.

"I'm so *proud* of you!" Isabelle said that night at dinner.

She had lit candles and put out fancy place mats to celebrate Arlie's triumph. And she had cooked something delicious, although when Michael had asked what it was, she'd told him it would taste better if he didn't know.

Isabelle, who had taken balloon rides and lived in Africa and hitchhiked across Europe all by herself, was proud of *Arlie*.

"It's no big deal," Arlie said.

"Can I see you be in a play?" Michael asked.

"I don't know," Arlie said. She really didn't want to talk about it.

"I'll sit next to Mom," Michael said, concentrating on not spilling the glass of milk he was hoisting to his lips.

Suddenly, she hated him. Like that day in the hospital

when he'd said "car crash." Everyone loved Michael: that's what people always said—what her mother said. But Arlie hated him. Maybe she had always hated him and she had never known it. It scared her how easy it was to hate someone. Her own little brother. She was supposed to love him most of all. Her mother had said to take care of him.

She felt Isabelle's eyes on her and flushed, as though Isabelle could see through her and know what she was really thinking.

"We'll all be there," Isabelle said, her hair glowing in the flickering light. "If we have to, we'll dress up as old people and *sneak* in."

"Yeah," Michael said, laughing a little.

Arlie knew they meant well, but it only reminded her how Isabelle wasn't afraid of anything, even of doing something she wasn't supposed to do. And how Michael didn't deserve to be hated. It wasn't his fault that he was loved the most.

That night in her sleeping bag, Arlie listened to the sounds outside the living room window. What if they weren't horns and tire skids and cabdrivers yelling? What if they were locusts, or unfamiliar footsteps in heavy underbrush, or the occasional roar of a drowsy lion? Arlie tried to imagine those things, tried to make her heart race in terror the way it had when she'd done nothing more than stand up in front of twenty-two kids she'd known almost her whole life.

The funny thing was, she didn't think sleeping on an African plain would frighten her nearly as much. Maybe, but she didn't think so.

She sighed and tried to think of something else. The

image of Casey Lane floated up in the darkness before her. Casey had made the audition worse somehow. Just her being there, watching, a witness to Arlie's terror. And telling her what to do. Still, even knowing all that, Arlie was over-come with wanting Casey to like *her.*

Liking someone and not liking her at the same time—it was the most confusing thing she'd ever felt. Too confusing, Arlie thought. She would never understand.

She let herself think of her mother. Sleeping. Always sleeping now. Did Mom dream in a coma? What did she dream about? Michael, probably. Clean closets; a neatly mown lawn. Things that made her happy.

A thought occurred to Arlie. What if her mother was dreaming about being a little girl again? What if Casey Lane was really just the product of her mother's imagination somehow let loose in Arlie's life? Arlie tried to concentrate, but it was simply too hard; in the end, she let the thought drift away. She felt guilty—she had to figure it out—but so far every solution to the mystery seemed only to lead to more questions, more impossibilities.

I won't give up, she thought, even as she noticed, with relief, that she had begun to fall toward sleep.

"We should practice together," Casey said to Arlie the next day at lunch.

Belinda and Xenia were sitting right there, but Casey had said it just to Arlie.

"Yeah, maybe," Arlie said. "All of us," she added.

She could see Belinda smiling, as though she was happy Arlie had remembered her.

"Oh . . . okay," Casey said unconvincingly.

"I don't think I need to practice that much," Xenia said. "I'm just the shoemaker. I only have a few lines."

"Yeah, but you need to know how a shoemaker *acts*. How she *behaves,*" Casey said.

"Shoemakers don't behave," Xenia said. "It's just a few lines."

Casey looked superior. "You could make it an interesting character if you really wanted," she said.

Xenia looked as though she was going to explode, but Belinda interrupted. "Maybe we could all get together after school today," she said.

Xenia shook her head. "I've got my rock-climbing class."

"And we're supposed to babysit," Arlie said to Belinda. "Remember?"

Oddly, she was glad for the chance to take care of Jesse Sweeney. It was familiar—something from her life before everything had gotten so strange and scary. It was comforting, like playing Go Fish at the hospital: a welcome distraction.

Belinda turned to Casey, and before Arlie could stop her, she asked, "You want to come babysit with us?"

"Sure," Casey said. "I love kids."

"You do?" Arlie was surprised.

Casey nodded. "Is it a boy or a girl?"

"A boy," Arlie said.

"Boys are easier than girls," Casey said. "I like boys more."

No surprise there. "How come they're easier?" Arlie asked.

"They do what you tell them," Casey said. "Girls are always arguing and asking you why. I don't get girls."

It's the first time she ever admitted not getting something, Arlie thought. "This boy never does what you tell him."

"You have to know *how* to tell him," Casey said. "But I have to go home first."

"That's okay," Belinda said. "Come to my house at ten to four. We can all walk over together."

"There's not going to be any time for practicing," Arlie said. "Jesse's a lot of work."

"Leave it to me," Casey said.

Again Arlie felt it: that crashing-together of wanting to impress Casey and not really trusting her, wonder and fear, liking and not liking.

"We can rehearse in front of him," Casey said. "It'll keep him occupied."

She smiled, clearly pleased to have thought of something efficient. But Arlie could tell that Belinda didn't like the way she was just taking over.

"Maybe this isn't such a good idea," Arlie said.

"It'll be fine," Casey said. "I'm good with boys. You'll see."

I know *that*, Arlie thought.

That wasn't the problem at all.

"Why did you invite her?" she asked Belinda later, during Quiet Talking.

"I guess I was just being polite," Belinda said.

Belinda was always being polite.

"She's kind of a pain," Arlie said. She just wanted to see if Belinda would agree.

"She's a *huge* pain," Belinda said. "Bossy and unfriendly, and she acts like she knows everything." She wrinkled her nose.

Arlie had never heard Belinda say so many mean things about someone all at the same time. "She did say she doesn't get girls," Arlie said. But she was thinking, Why am I defending her?

"Maybe because she just goes around *ignoring* what they're saying. Ignoring that they're even *standing* there," Belinda said.

"She doesn't do that. Exactly."

"Yes, she does. Except to you," Belinda said. "She pays a lot of attention to you."

Was Belinda jealous of Casey? Impossible. Belinda knew that she was Arlie's best friend, that not even Xenia—who'd brought Arlie a snickerdoodle every day in second grade— was a threat.

Still. Arlie knew what it was like not to be sure. "I wish you hadn't invited her," she said. "It's more fun when it's just us."

Belinda looked grateful. "Maybe it'll be all right," she said doubtfully. "Maybe putting on a play for Jesse will work out."

"Yeah," Arlie said, her heart sinking in her chest like a rock. "Maybe."

As it turned out, trying to put on a play for Jesse was not a great idea. In fact, it was a terrible idea. Maybe, Arlie thought, the most terrible idea Casey Lane had ever had.

"What's a play?" Jesse had asked crankily after Mrs. Sweeney had left. He was already fussy.

"It's like telling a story," Casey explained. "Only not from a book. It's like watching TV."

Jesse brightened somewhat.

"Only *not* TV," Belinda said. But it was too late.

"I want to watch cartoons," Jesse said.

"You're not allowed to," Arlie said.

Jesse glared at her. "You're not my mom," he said. "You're not even supposed to be here."

"What do you mean, I'm not supposed to be here?" Arlie asked. "I'm here every week."

"I told my mom I hate you," Jesse said. "I told her to make you stop coming. I want it to be just her." Her pointed at Belinda. Arlie wondered if he even knew their names.

Belinda knelt down in front of Jesse and grabbed his hands. His sweaty, smelly, cereal-crumb-covered hands. Had Michael's hands been like that when he was four? If they had been, Arlie was sure she never would have touched him, no matter how funny he was.

"Hey, come on, big guy," Belinda said.

"You're not supposed to watch cartoons, right, Jesse?" Casey asked, her arms folded on her chest, sounding measured and reasonable, like a teacher instead of a girl.

A teacher or a mom.

"Who *is* that?" Jesse asked.

Before Belinda could answer, Casey said, "Jesse? Are you supposed to watch cartoons?"

"You're not supposed to be asking me stuff," Jesse whined. He removed one of his hands from Belinda's and rubbed his eye hard.

"Jesse." Casey stared at him until he looked at her, his mouth sagging open slightly, both hands dropping to his sides.

When he still didn't answer, she said, "Can you hear me?"

He nodded. Casey's voice was calm—almost quiet— but for some reason Arlie felt herself growing more and more nervous, as though there were a lot of yelling going on.

"Then you need to answer me," Casey said. "Are you supposed to watch cartoons or not?"

Jesse's face was starting to turn red. "No," he whispered.

Casey looked triumphant. Suddenly, she didn't look anything like a teacher or a mom. She looked like a kid who'd beaten someone at a video game or been praised by a teacher for neat handwriting.

"Then sit down on the couch," she said. "And be quiet. And we'll put on our play. You can be the audience," she added, her first effort at trying to make it sound like something fun.

But when Jesse didn't move, she reached down to take his arm in her hand—not hard, Arlie could see, just firmly enough to lead him over to the couch. At her touch, Jesse began to wail.

Arlie had never heard anything like it. Like some kind of jungle animal, maybe, that hadn't even been discovered yet. Or like the way a fire alarm would sound in your head after you'd swallowed it.

"Oh, Jesse," Belinda begged, still on her knees. "Oh, sweetie!"

"Come on, Jesse. Quit it," Arlie said, raising her voice to be heard over the howling.

Only Casey seemed unperturbed. She reached again for Jesse's arm. This time, he yanked it away from her—his wail rising to the level of a shriek—and she put her arms around him from behind and picked him up, holding him to her chest, ignoring his flailing sandaled feet. She walked awkwardly to the couch and tried to deposit him there, but Jesse, sensing defeat, stiffened in defiance and rage. Tears streaked down his fat red cheeks, and snot bubbled from his nose. He looked completely disgusting.

Undeterred, Casey bent over him. Her body hid him from Arlie's view, but when Casey stood up, Jesse was sitting on the couch. Seeing her rise, he once again went rigid, his whole body straightening and slipping partway off the couch to the floor. Casey, whose face had begun to gleam with sweat, leaned over again and hauled the sobbing, sticky boy back to an upright position. She rested one hand on his shoulder, and this time he stayed put.

Arlie and Belinda watched, openmouthed.

"You just have to be firm," Casey said. She was a little out of breath, something Arlie found satisfying.

Jesse was now hiccupping through his sobs. His arms were covered with tears and snot as he rubbed them across his swollen eyes.

"We kind of try not to get him too upset," Belinda whispered.

"Why?" Casey asked.

"What do you mean 'why'?" Arlie said. "Because of *this*. Because he gets like *this*!"

Casey shrugged. "Well, he's stopped now, hasn't he?"

"Yeah, but—"

"You just have to let him know who's boss," Casey said, wiping her hands on her skirt. From the couch, Jesse eyed her with equal parts terror and disbelief.

Arlie almost laughed out loud. She'd known it was coming. She felt something lighten in her chest. It was her mom, right here in the room with her, telling her things, just like always. To stand straight. To be firm.

But how? And why? Was this a miracle? Was the universe

trying to speak to her, tell her something? And if so, what?

"What if he tells his mom?" Belinda whispered again.

"Tells her what? That he was pitching a fit and we got him to stop? Without hitting him or punishing him or making him go to his room?" Casey turned to Jesse. "Hey. You want a cookie or something?"

Jesse nodded.

Casey turned to Arlie and Belinda and smiled. She looked exhausted. "I think I'm losing my mind," she said.

Arlie simply waited.

"What little is *left* of my mind," Casey added.

In the kitchen, Belinda said to Arlie, "I don't think she knows very much about kids."

She said it calmly, but Arlie knew she was furious.

"I could have gotten him to stop screaming," Belinda said, pouring milk carefully into a plastic cup. "I could have done it *nicely*."

"I know," Arlie said. "You're nice to him."

Too nice, maybe.

"I don't think she should have come in here acting like she knows how to do everything," Belinda whispered. "She *is* new."

Arlie didn't say anything. This is how it is for Casey, she thought, following Belinda back out to the living room. Wherever she goes. This is how people act when she tries to take over. No one likes her. Not even Belinda, who likes everyone.

Arlie didn't like her, either. But it made her sad to think that no one did.

Casey was putting coffee-table books into a perfect

stack. She looked up and smiled as Arlie and Belinda entered the room. "Where'd you put your scripts?" she asked.

The rehearsal was a disaster. Not two minutes into the girls' reading, Jesse again began to squirm and cry, and Casey was again forced to show him who was boss. It seemed to Arlie that she shouldn't have to do that a second time, let alone a third and a fourth.

"This isn't going to work," Belinda said when Jesse had slithered onto the floor a fifth time and lay sprawled and red-faced and weepy under the coffee table. "He knows you're going to stop and talk to him," she said to Casey. "He's *waiting* for you down there."

"You just have to keep doing it," Casey said, setting her script on the table and making her way to Jesse's half-prone form. "Eventually, he'll get tired and stop."

"Why don't you just sit with him and listen to *us* read?" Arlie asked.

"No," Casey said firmly, the merest hint of frustration creeping into her tone. "He has to learn."

Learn what? Arlie thought. For someone who didn't have brothers or sisters of her own, Casey was awfully sure she was right. And completely unwilling to admit she was wrong.

Which didn't surprise Arlie in the slightest.

eight

Arlie memorized her part in a couple of days. She practiced with Isabelle after dinner, and she and Belinda fed each other lines over the phone. When she was sure she knew her part cold, she felt a glimmer of pride and pleasure, but it was quickly doused with fear. In her secret heart, she had hoped that learning her lines would ease her terror at having to perform the play before the residents of the Leisure Valley Retirement Community.

Now that she could recite her part in her sleep, though, she knew that she would never be able to stand before them and act.

She couldn't bear to see Isabelle's disappointment; couldn't bear to hear Belinda's best-friend support. But the pressure of not telling anyone was welling up inside her, along with fear itself.

One night, when Isabelle was on the phone with the hospital, Arlie asked Michael, "What makes you scared?"

"The big boys at school," Michael said without hesitation. "The ones who say they'll flush your head down the toilet if you try and go to the bathroom at recess."

"They're not supposed to say that. Who says that?" For one moment, she forgot her own fear.

"Harrison Westover. He's in fourth grade. I think he has a beard."

"He doesn't have a beard. You should tell Ms. Guthrie."

"She won't do anything. She says you shouldn't tell on people."

"She means for stupid stuff. You should tell her about this."

Michael shrugged. "Maybe."

"No, really, Michael. You should. She'll do something. She'll make it stop."

Michael turned his attention back to the race car he'd been vrooming along the edge of the kitchen table.

"Michael?" Arlie waited until his eyes met hers. "You should."

"Stop telling me what to do," he said, cutting his eyes away. "Mom's the only one who can say 'should.'"

Arlie thought about this. Their mom was always saying "should." "Michael, you should go outside and play." "Arlie, you really should read the newspaper once in a while." It had always bugged her.

She'd never known that it bugged Michael, too.

"I hate when she does that," she said.

Michael looked at her. "You shouldn't say you hate her," he said. "Because she's sick."

"I didn't say I hate her," Arlie said. "I don't hate her."

Michael looked back down at his car. "I hate her," he whispered.

He looked so sad. Not the way he looked when one of his block towers fell. Sadder than she'd ever seen him. Her heart ached.

"No, you don't," she said. "You don't hate her."

"Yes, I do. And Dad, too." His knuckles were white from clutching the car so hard. "Why don't they call us?"

"Dad has a tube down his throat, for breathing. He can't

talk. And Mom—" She paused. "Mom can't talk right now, either."

They didn't say anything for a while.

"You *don't* hate her," Arlie said again.

"It feels like hating," Michael said.

She thought guiltily of that day in the hospital, and the night after she'd gotten the part: the times she'd hated Michael. Or thought she did. "I know," she said. "But it isn't."

After a moment, Michael sighed. "I wish there was a TV here," he said.

She knew what he meant. Sometimes you just didn't want to think anymore.

"You know this play I'm in at school?" she asked.

He nodded.

"I don't want to do it," Arlie said, lowering her voice.

"Why not?" Michael vroomed the race car some more. "Girls always want to do plays."

"I'm scared," Arlie whispered. "To stand up in front of everybody."

"Tell Mrs. Rubio."

Arlie was disappointed. She'd thought maybe Michael would know the answer.

"That won't help. She'll just make me do it."

Michael made the car travel down the table leg to the floor. "Tell her you'll do something awful if she makes you. Tell her you'll pick your nose until it bleeds."

Clearly, Michael was going to be no help at all.

"I saw Walter do that once. Blood got all over his shirt and everything," Michael said from the floor. "It was cool."

Arlie rose. "Thanks anyway."

"Hey," Michael said. Arlie couldn't see his head, hidden beneath the tabletop. "I guess it's not really hating."

Arlie smiled. "I know it's not."

"I don't get it."

"I know," Arlie said. She knew exactly what "it" was: everything. "I don't, either."

She could hear the sounds of the race car's tires buzzing as Michael shoved them forward and back over the faded purple rug.

She waited, but he didn't say anything more. Arlie felt the way she did on rainy days, looking out past the drippy windowpane at the puddles on the lawn. Maybe there were no answers, nothing to get. Maybe it was just endless gloom, for no reason, because the universe felt like it.

She thought she heard a stifled sob.

"I know one thing," she said, kicking lightly at Michael's elbow with her foot. "You have to keep trying to figure it out."

"I'm sick of trying," Michael said after a minute.

"I know," Arlie said. "But I think that's what you're supposed to do."

No answer.

"Mom would like for us to keep trying," she said softly.

Later, when Michael had fallen asleep and Isabelle was cleaning Elizabeth's cage, Arlie sat alone in the living room. Even in the near-dark of candlelight, Isabelle's kitchen and living room had begun to seem more familiar than her own house, her own room. She thought about her bed: the bottom bunk strewn with red and pink pillows, made with a bright red quilt and candy-striped sheets, the top bunk, where she slept and read, neater, less cluttered. She always kept her current book tucked under the pillow. *Heidi* was still there; she had forgotten to pack it when they'd come to Isabelle's.

From the top bunk, she could look down on the shelves neatly lined with books and picture frames. Several frames sat on her desk as well: one with a photo of her and Belinda posing in front of Belinda's trampoline, one with her and Dad at the top of Mount Diablo. That had been a fun day. They had climbed on the huge, smooth rocks with holes the size of closets, carved with the initials of people who had come before them. Arlie had found her own initials—AEM—etched in a rock over "1967." In celebration, they had eaten their picnic lunch atop that boulder, and when an elderly couple passed by on the trail, her father had asked them to take their picture. He did that a lot—talked to strangers, made friends with people he didn't know: the telephone operator, the man who took their money at the tollbooth.

Until this moment, Arlie hadn't thought much about him; she had forgotten him a little, with all the worrying she'd been doing about her mom.

How could you ever figure anything out when there was always something new to feel awful about?

"You aren't going to believe this," Belinda said, running up to Arlie on the playground. Around them, kids ran and shrieked, trying to get in a lot of playing before the 8:15 bell.

"What?"

"We got fired."

"*What?*"

"Mrs. Sweeney called. She said she was sorry, and to tell you, too. She didn't know how to reach you at Isabelle's."

Belinda glanced from side to side, making sure she wasn't heard, not wanting anyone to know of their humiliation. "She said Jesse told her mean stuff about us."

"What stuff?"

"Oh, I don't know," Belinda said miserably. "Who knows what he would say? That *we* were mean, maybe. I don't know."

"*Us? Mean?*" This was unbelievable. "Me, maybe. I can be mean. But you?"

"You aren't mean, either. Just—" Belinda paused. "Strict."

The bell rang and kids around them began to scurry. "This absolutely stinks," Arlie said, trying to force herself to think clearly. "How am I going to pay for Architectural Drawing?"

She meant it when she said it, but she was thinking that she would really miss the routine, the familiarity of babysitting Jesse Sweeney.

"How am I going to tell my mom?" Belinda whispered, her eyes glistening.

After a moment, she reached for Arlie's arm. "I'm sorry," she said.

"It's okay."

"No. I didn't mean it. I wasn't thinking."

"It's okay," Arlie said again. "You didn't do anything wrong."

They didn't say anything after that. But they both knew how much worse it was when there was no one to be disappointed in you, no one to tell.

"We got fired," Arlie said matter-of-factly at lunch.

"Wow," Casey said.

"Arlie was saving up for drawing class," Belinda explained. "I was just doing it for fun."

"Wow," Casey said again. "That's too bad."

"I mean, it wasn't exactly the best job in the world. It wasn't exactly fun," Belinda went on. "Not with Jesse being the way he is. But I liked it anyway."

Casey chewed and swallowed, nodding.

One of Mom's favorite expressions was "cool as a cucumber." It popped into Arlie's head as she watched Casey chewing and swallowing and nodding, saying nothing.

But later, when Belinda hissed, "*She*'s the one who got us fired, I bet," as they were lining up to go back to class, a perverse sense of wanting to be fair made Arlie say, "Probably not."

"She had something to do with it, anyway," Belinda said. "I don't like her. I don't trust her."

Arlie felt an unfamiliar pang: pity for her mom. She had never thought of Mom as someone people didn't like. Her father loved her. And Michael. And the people she worked with. But now that Arlie thought about it, she had no friends. A few women who called and asked for volunteers for PTA phone-a-thons, and one or two she mentioned from her aerobics class. But they seemed more like acquaintances, people she just occasionally bumped into. Not real friends.

Was it because of all the moving around she'd done when she was a kid? Was she afraid, even now, that she'd have to move, have to leave people behind? That making friends wasn't worth the trouble?

"Maybe," she said to Belinda, "we're jumping to conclusions."

Belinda shook her head more firmly than Arlie had ever

seen her. "You'll see," she said. "From now on, I'm staying away from that girl."

It was almost a threat, as if she were saying "And you should, too."

"It won't hurt to have lunch with her once in a while," Arlie said.

"Well," Belinda said as they crossed the threshold of Room 22, "I'll sit on another bench, then."

Even though it was only the end of March, the next morning dawned hot. It was the first really hot day of the year. Mrs. Rubio gave a spelling quiz and went over multiplication by eights. She sent Amanda Bordman to the office for talking and confiscated Jeremy Sanchez's drawing of Abraham Lincoln throwing up into his hat. Everyone was bored. No one raised a hand or even asked a question, and for once Mrs. Rubio didn't seem to care. Even lunch recess was slow. By then the sun glared overhead, and the hydrangea bushes lining the schoolyard looked brittle and brown. It was hard to move, hard to breathe. Arlie wanted a drink, but the water always ran hot out of the fountain, and she didn't want to walk over to it anyway.

The day dragged on. Mrs. Rubio showed a video about California agriculture, and Arlie was so bored that she dozed off. She jerked awake when her chin touched her chest, afraid she'd been drooling or making a funny noise. She licked her fingertips and rubbed them across her eyelids, hoping the cooling air would keep her awake. Around her, the classroom ticked and buzzed with the sleepy sounds of afternoon.

"You want to come over?" Belinda asked when the bell rang. "Xenia's coming. We're going to do origami."

"Sounds fun," Arlie said, "but I can't."

She didn't want to tell Belinda what she was doing. Or Isabelle or Michael, either, for that matter.

"Xenia says she can teach me how to make a penguin," Belinda said. "And we're going to make strawberry slushies."

She wanted to go—slushies sounded good—but she said no and left school alone, head down, shoulders squared against the heat.

She walked in the direction of home—her real home, her house, where she really lived. She was surprised to find herself missing it. As she moved slowly along the familiar sidewalks, she felt the closest thing to homesickness she had ever known. It was hard to say what she missed: not so much the house itself. Just the feeling of living somewhere, of calling someplace home. She thought of Casey and her boxes: her glass fish, wrapped in tissue and old newspaper, untouchable.

It had been three weeks since they had gone to stay with Isabelle.

Arlie turned onto her street. The houses looked at once the same and different, like a place she had seen a picture of but never visited. She knew every crack in the sidewalk, every tree root, every crooked fence post and dented mailbox. Two doors away from her house, she paused, suddenly afraid that she would be overcome with the desire to go inside. Like when she'd been little, and her father had let her sit in a life-sized plastic car at Toys "R" Us, then tried to coax her out. She had screamed frantically and caused a scene, wanting what she couldn't have.

Steeling herself, she walked the last few feet. The house looked slightly shabby: the lawn needed mowing. Ronnie

Glazer from up the street was supposed to be taking care of it. He was in high school and was always getting in trouble for banging up the car. Arlie thought his head was too big, but that might have been because he shaved it.

She stood on the sidewalk, just looking, hoping the neighbors weren't watching. Did her house look abandoned? She imagined the windows were eyes, and then it did seem to stare at her, as if slightly ashamed of being unkempt. But abandoned? No. Someone lived there. A family lived there. She didn't know how, but she could tell, and she was glad.

Turning away, she thought that it wasn't just that the house was hers. *She* belonged to *it*, even when she was away for a long time. And this fact of belonging was part of her. She would be a different person without it.

Arlie headed back the way she had come. But instead of turning toward Isabelle's, she went the other way, glancing over each shoulder, feeling a little silly but not wanting to be noticed. The air seemed to shimmer. Nothing moved. Her breathing was the loudest sound in the thick heat.

She stopped when she could make out the Sweeneys' front door. There was a tree across the street: she stood behind it, pretending to examine its bark, not wanting to look as though she was really hiding. The leaves above her provided a skimpy canopy. She remembered running home once in a February rain, the thin, leafless trees offering little cover.

She knew things about the people who lived in these houses, even if she didn't really know the people. Mrs. Krasner, who lived in a turquoise house next door to the Sweeneys, had adult children who never visited her. Mrs. Sweeney liked to invite her over for coffee; "She's a dear,"

Mrs. Sweeney was always saying, even though Arlie could tell that she wished Mrs. Krasner would paint her house another color.

The Bellamys lived in the corner house; Mr. Bellamy was on the town council, and Arlie's dad was always calling him about things like easements and zoning ordinances. Then he'd get off the phone and tell Mom how he wasn't voting for Mr. Bellamy the next time around because he was a complete idiot. And Mom would say how she'd heard that Mrs. Bellamy was getting a little too familiar with the pool man. She would lower her voice when she said it, trying to make sure Arlie didn't hear, and Arlie would wonder how you could be *too* familiar. Why was it embarrassing to her mother? Why didn't her mother know that you were supposed to *want* to be familiar with people?

Maybe, Arlie thought now, because when her mother was a girl, she'd never lived anywhere long enough to memorize the cracks in the sidewalk, to know with her eyes closed which houses had dented mailboxes.

She heard a car turning onto the street and froze as it drove slowly past her, then turned again at the stop sign. It was Mrs. Bishop's beat-up Volvo. Mrs. Bishop had a son named Hector, who wore black cloaks to high school and listened to music that sounded, according to Mrs. Bishop, like jungle parrots being fed into a wood chipper. Mrs. Bishop had told Mom that she'd asked Hector if he was ready to wear something besides black cloaks, which were expensive to clean. When Hector said no, she told him that he was going to have to pay for his own dry cleaning, even if it meant bagging groceries, and when Hector told her that grocery clerks didn't wear black cloaks, she told him to stuff it.

Arlie heard footsteps; she tried to make herself look small behind the tree trunk. It was rough against her face, and smelled of earth. Peeking around, she saw what she had known she would see, what she had been afraid to see. She saw Casey Lane heading up the Sweeneys' front walk.

She watched as Casey walked toward the door, the ends of her hair bobbing slightly, her thin sundress barely fluttering around her knees. In the heavy heat, she looked strangely comfortable, as though she were cooled by a fan that blew inside her. From her post, Arlie couldn't see Casey's face, but she knew that her expression would be clear and unworried, without the trace of a smile or frown to give away her thoughts.

She watched as Casey pushed the doorbell, then stepped back. Watched as Mrs. Sweeney opened the door and stood aside, allowing Casey to enter. Arlie imagined the air-conditioned hallway, the embrace of coolness, and knew, just knew, that Casey wouldn't feel a thing.

"It was you," Arlie said into the phone that night.

She sat on the floor of Isabelle's purple and yellow bathroom, the cordless phone tucked against her ear, her hands roaming in the shaggy dampness of the bath mat. She tried to keep her voice low; she didn't want Isabelle or Michael to overhear. Living in an apartment with people around was a big, fat pain.

"What are you talking about?" Casey asked.

"You know exactly what I'm talking about," Arlie said. "You got us fired."

"That," Casey said, "is ridiculous."

Arlie wasn't buying it for a minute.

"You called Mrs. Sweeney," she went on. "You told her Jesse hated us, or that we made him cry. Something."

"You're crazy," Casey said.

"Maybe you told Jesse a lie about us when Belinda and I weren't looking. When we were in the kitchen. That we eat kids who don't behave. That we stick pins in them while they take their naps."

"I didn't do any such thing."

"Then how come I saw you going to the Sweeneys' house this afternoon?"

There was a small silence.

"Well," Casey said, "I did go to the Sweeneys' house." She sounded almost guilty.

"To babysit, right?"

"Yes."

"I *knew* it."

"But I didn't get you fired. I—"

"Belinda was *good* at that job," Arlie said hotly. "Better than you. She hugged that kid when he was screaming and covered with snot and sticky crumbs. She played Chutes and Ladders with him and never let him know she knew he was cheating. She let him win, even."

"But—"

"All Jesse had to do was scrunch his face up. He didn't even really have to cry. He just had to look like he was *going* to cry and Belinda would hug him."

She was overcome with the strangest feeling: the knowledge that her own mother was now, in addition to everything else, a liar.

"Being a good babysitter doesn't mean hugging all the time," Casey said in a know-it-all voice.

"I can see how Mrs. Sweeney might want to get rid of me," Arlie said. She pulled hard at a strand of the purple rug. "But it's totally not fair about Belinda."

Again, there was silence.

"It's rotten, actually," Arlie said, clicking the phone off, this time not even waiting to see if Casey would say anything.

That night, lying on the floor in her sleeping bag while Michael dozed and Isabelle read aloud quietly from *A Tale of Two Cities,* she couldn't get Casey out of her mind.

"Isabelle?"

Isabelle set the book down on her lap and smiled. Earlier she had talked to the nurse, who had said that Arlie's dad was going to get his breathing tube taken out tomorrow.

Arlie's mom hadn't changed, though. "No change," Isabelle had told Arlie, and then, "Sometimes that's a good thing."

Now she said, "You don't have to understand every word. Just listen."

Arlie shook her head. "Not that."

"What then?" Isabelle said.

"Did Mom ever lie?"

Isabelle pulled a loose strand of curly red hair away from her face. "What do you mean?"

"Well, you know—lie. About anything."

Isabelle seemed to consider this. "No, bunny. Not once, that I can remember."

Arlie nodded in the half-light. It was reassuring and terrible at the same time.

"Now that you mention it, I'd have to say that she's a

remarkably truthful person. Maybe too truthful sometimes," Isabelle said.

That was what Arlie had always thought, too, until that
day. Or hadn't thought, had just *known*, because it had never
occurred to her that her mother *would* lie.

"I mean, how many times do you really need to be told
that your hair needs combing?" Isabelle smiled at Arlie. "It
wouldn't hurt your mother to lie just a *little*. Just once in a
while."

Arlie was so tired that she felt her eyelids drooping, like
petals on a flower at dusk. "But she wouldn't," she heard
herself say. "She just wouldn't."

She was too close to sleep to let herself think about what
this really meant.

nine

Mrs. Rubio let the class practice *Who's Minding the Store?* for half an hour every afternoon before the three o'clock bell. Slowly, slowly, the play began to take shape. All the kids started to remember their lines, even the boys who didn't want anyone to think they actually cared about being in a play. "Look up! Look up!" Mrs. Rubio called when Amanda Bordman said her lines to the floor, and eventually Amanda remembered and raised her head without being reminded. Even Jeremy seemed to be trying harder; he no longer tried to get milk to run out of his nose while he was supposed to be pretending to sweep the sidewalk.

For her part, Arlie knew her lines cold, but that was little comfort. No matter how many times she said them, she could not shake the feeling of dread that seeped into her bones when she stood before the class as Petey. Her palms sweated and itched. A funny noise—like summer frogs croaking in the drainage ditch—buzzed in her ears. Her cheeks turned red, as though she had sat in the sun too long. And when rehearsal was over for the day, her head throbbed and she ached with relief.

Stage fright, she knew it was called. Frage stight, she thought, sad that she couldn't tell Belinda without confessing to her how afraid she was. Arlie was always the brave one, just like Belinda was always the nice one. Telling Belinda how scared she was would upset the balance of things, would make everything strange and rickety between them, and Arlie didn't want to do that. Things were strange enough.

Still, even with the daily deluge of fear, she found she had begun to enjoy watching the boys in her class, just to see how they did things differently. It was amazing, when she really paid attention. Boys sucked their sleeves while they watched Mrs. Rubio explain fractions; girls never did that. They hit each other all the time, even when they liked each other. They thought it was funny to put barbecue sauce on grapes and eat them. They were loud, even when they were trying not to be.

"Why are you so loud?" she asked Warren one day while they stood in line waiting to be seated in the auditorium for an assembly about not smoking. "Why don't boys ever talk without yelling?"

Around them, kids from all the grades were shouting and laughing. The teachers were trying to keep everyone quiet and rolling their eyes at each other when they thought no one was looking. "Bedlam," her mother would have said.

"Girls yell, too," Warren said. "Look at Mrs. Rubio."

"Yeah, but she's just trying to be heard. Boys can't be quiet, even when they're trying."

"I guess you're right. Boys don't whisper much. Girls are always whispering." Warren shoved his hands in his pockets as they moved forward. "It makes me nervous."

"I know what you mean."

"If I knew why, it wouldn't be so bad," Warren said. "But with girls, you never do."

As a girl herself, Arlie felt as though she was being called upon to explain. "Sometimes it's secrets, but not always. Sometimes it's just—" She paused, not knowing how to say it.

"See?" Warren said. "You don't know, either. No one knows."

"Someone does. Just not me," Arlie said. "It's like adding fractions. Just because I can't do it doesn't mean someone else can't."

Warren shook his head firmly. "Adding fractions is impossible," he said. "It can't be done."

"That's dumb," Arlie said. "*Someone* knows how."

For a split second, the auditorium hushed: in one moment, there was near-quiet where before there had been sound. It was one of those freaky things that happened sometimes, inexplicably, as though all the kids had taken a breath at the exact same time.

"I like knowing," Arlie said as the noise started back up again. "Figuring things out." She looked at Warren. "You can ask Mrs. Rubio for help with fractions, you know. There *is* an answer."

Warren shrugged. "Not always." With the rest of the class, they walked down a row of empty seats and sat. "No one knows about the whispering and the yelling."

"Maybe someone does," Arlie said. "Maybe just not us."

But as the auditorium lights dimmed, she had a feeling that Warren was right, that there were some things that no one could understand, ever. Why boys were different from girls. Why people did mean things to each other. Jeremy Sanchez. Moms.

"It's *Bart Blodgett Explains the Mysteries of the Universe!*" Michael shrieked.

Isabelle was taking them out to dinner for the first time since the night they had gone to Mel's for French fries. She had run out of ideas for meals, she explained, which Arlie didn't really believe. Isabelle never ran out of ideas for anything. Probably she had just forgotten to go to the store.

They had been walking up Malverne to Isabelle's favorite vegetarian burrito stand when Michael caught sight of a small electronics store. In the front window, a row of TVs was tuned to the same channel. On the screens, a man wearing thick black-framed glasses and a white lab coat was pouring liquid into a steaming glass beaker.

Isabelle made a siren noise. "Nine-one-one? Send the fashion police *immediately.*"

"He's really cool," Michael said, mesmerized by the four identical images of Bart Blodgett. "He explains about volcanoes and the Bermuda Triangle and armadillos and sea horses."

"What about sea horses?" Isabelle asked.

"The boys have the eggs."

"He means the *males carry* the eggs," Arlie explained to Isabelle.

"They do not!" Isabelle said indignantly. "That's impossible."

Arlie knew she was kidding. Working at a wildlife museum, Isabelle knew this kind of stuff.

"Uh-huh!" Michael said, his eyes big with certainty. "Bart Blodgett says."

"Is there any difference between a mystery of the universe and a freak of nature?" Isabelle asked, just to tease.

Was there?

"'Mystery of the universe' sounds prettier," Arlie said. "'Freak of nature' is when something's just weird, or icky, or maybe a little sickening."

"Like you!" Michael laughed and pointed at her. He clutched his stomach, laughing. It was the first time Arlie had heard him really laugh, in the old way, since the car accident. She realized that she had missed it.

"And irritating, right, Isabelle?" she said, turning away from Michael so he wouldn't see her smile. "Freaks of nature are always incredibly irritating, right?"

"Right," Isabelle said. "Nothing is as irritating as a pregnant male sea horse."

But while they were waiting for their burritos, Arlie remembered Mr. Cunningham when he'd given her the mirror for Christmas. "All that beauty and the beholder stuff," he'd said. "Don't you forget it."

She knew he meant that something ugly to one person could be beautiful to another. "That's just something people say to make you feel better if you have a big nose, or hair that won't stay combed," she said.

Mr. Cunningham had laughed. "It's about how you look at things," he said. "Don't let other people tell you what's what. Keep an open mind. Not so open that everything falls out," he added. "Just open enough."

"Ajar," Arlie had added, making him laugh again.

Now she said to Isabelle, "Maybe one person's freak is another person's mystery."

Isabelle reached around Arlie's shoulders and pulled her close. "What a wise little bunny you are, bunny," she said, as if she was really proud.

Arlie smiled, even though she knew she wasn't wise. Not

really. But she vowed to remember to keep an open mind. You never knew when *that* might come in handy.

They stuffed themselves with broccoli-carrot-garlic burritos. Even Michael, who had once seen a cartoon about aliens with thousands of tiny eye-stalks on their heads. Broccoli-heads, they had been called. He had tried explaining it to Mom, who had pressed her lips together and said he had to take three bites of broccoli anyway. It had been eight o'clock before she had finally taken his plate away and let him leave the table, hungry but victorious.

After dinner, Isabelle rushed them out the door and down the street toward her apartment. Michael wanted to linger at the store with the TVs, but Isabelle said there wasn't time.

"Time for what?" Arlie asked, but Isabelle said nothing, just planted her hands on Michael's and Arlie's backs and gently shoved them onward.

The phone was ringing as Isabelle fumbled with her keys in the hall. Suddenly, Arlie knew—just knew, with a mysterious certainty—and as Isabelle pushed open the front door, she lurched toward the phone.

"Hello? Dad?" she yelled into the receiver.

"Hey, pumpkin!" He sounded faraway and raspy and weak. But otherwise the same. Arlie's heart raced with happiness. Then she burst into tears.

"Oh, pumpkin," her dad said over and over. "Stop. Please."

He was begging her, but she couldn't. Briefly, it occurred to her that if it were her mother asking her to stop crying, she would have dug down deep inside herself, would have found a way.

Finally, her sobbing subsided, and Dad said feebly, "Everything's going to be all right, sweetie. Really. It is."

"What about Mom?"

For a minute, her father didn't say anything. Then he sighed. "Arlie," he said, "all we can do is wait and think good thoughts."

More waiting. "I *am* thinking good thoughts," she said.

"That's my pumpkin. How's school? You holding up?"

She nodded, then whispered, "It's okay."

"You doing your homework?"

She sighed. "Yes, Dad."

She tried to think of something to say and couldn't. It was hard making conversation with someone in the hospital.

"How are your fingers?" she asked.

What her mother would have asked.

Her dad laughed. "They'll be okay," he said. "Everything will be okay."

She tried to believe him.

"Hey," her father whispered. His voice sounded tired and used up. "Can I talk to Michael?"

Arlie looked around the room. Michael had run into Isabelle's bedroom when Arlie had started crying. "Michael!" she yelled.

No answer.

"Michael!" Isabelle went to the bedroom door and cracked it open. "Come talk to your daddy."

"I'm busy," Michael said.

Isabelle shut the door gently. "Let me talk to him," she said, walking toward Arlie, her hand outstretched for the phone.

Arlie handed it over. "Hey, goofball," she heard Isabelle

say, as if this were just a regular phone call, as if her dad had simply forgotten to pack his cymbals and was asking Isabelle to ship them overnight.

Isabelle was nodding and smiling into the phone, looking up every once in a while at Arlie with a hopeful arch in her eyebrows. "Okay, big guy," she said a couple of times. Finally, she said, "Call tomorrow night. He'll talk to you tomorrow," and Arlie could see that her eyes were sparkling with tears.

When she hung up, they just looked at each other.

"See?" Isabelle said at last. "He's better. He's getting better."

"Not Mom, though."

"We don't know that," Isabelle said.

"Well, she's still in a coma," Arlie said, feeling angry, and sick of Isabelle for being wishy-washy and optimistic. "People in a coma aren't 'better.'"

Isabelle didn't say anything.

"Maybe they're not even in there anymore," Arlie added.

Isabelle said, "She's in there."

"Don't say 'She's resting'!" Arlie screamed. Trying to compose herself, she added, "And don't say 'Everything will be okay.'"

Isabelle nodded, her eyes trained hard on Arlie's.

They just sat there.

Finally, Isabelle said, "You want to talk to Michael, or should I?"

Arlie rose from the table. "I'll do it," she said, even though, as she opened the bedroom door, she had no idea what she was going to say.

***

In the end, she didn't say anything. She walked to where Michael sat in front of Elizabeth's terrarium, watching with his chin on his arm. There wasn't much to see: Elizabeth sat nearly motionless, occasionally raising a hairy orange leg. As if she were waving, signaling that she knew they were there and she appreciated their attention. It was oddly soothing.

Arlie pulled up a chair and sat down. Michael glanced over at her, then back at Elizabeth. Normally, he would have said something about her sitting too close, fogging up the terrarium, breathing all the good air. Arlie knew that by not saying anything he was saying it was okay for her to be there, that he was glad for her nearness.

They watched Elizabeth for almost an hour, until Isabelle came in and gently reminded them of bedtime.

Mrs. Rubio was getting frantic.

"One week! One measly week!" she yelled the next Friday when Curtis Little flubbed his lines three times in a row. "How are you going to perform at Leisure Valley if you don't know your lines?"

Curtis blushed and looked at the floor.

"It's not just you, Curtis," Mrs. Rubio said. "Several of you are on very thin ice here. You don't know your lines. You don't speak loudly, the way we've practiced. You don't get off the stage when you're supposed to. How is that going to look?"

"Retarded," Jeremy Sanchez said.

Mrs. Rubio glared at him. She didn't like kids to say "retarded."

"It does not look good," she said coldly. "It looks terrible. It's embarrassing. You are embarrassing me."

The class was silent.

"You are embarrassing yourselves," Mrs. Rubio said.

Everyone—even Jeremy—looked glum.

"You can behave like baboons at home. I don't care. But I do care when you act silly and . . . and . . . *ignorant* in public!"

Mrs. Rubio never said "ignorant" unless she was really mad.

"So." She took a deep breath and smoothed the front of her pants over her stomach. "Get yourselves together. Figure out a way to make this right." The bell rang. "Do yourselves proud," she finished, like somebody trying to get elected.

At lunch, everyone was talking about it.

"It was like a temper tantrum," Belinda said. "Like Jesse. Remember?" she added wistfully.

Arlie nodded. "Only Jesse didn't say words like 'ignorant,'" she said. "Mostly he just screamed and turned red."

Belinda's eyes got misty. Arlie could tell how much she missed him. Unbelievable, she thought.

"I think she was mainly talking to Jeremy and Curtis and those boys," Xenia said.

"Did I do all right?" Arlie asked. She tried to sound casual.

"You were fine," Xenia said.

Arlie was relieved. When she read her lines, she was so shaky and scared that she couldn't tell what she looked like or how she sounded. She had been afraid that Mrs. Rubio had been talking specifically to her.

Casey Lane walked past their bench. She didn't look at them or smile. She walked over to the main hallway and disappeared.

"How come she doesn't sit with us anymore?" Xenia said.

Belinda shrugged. "She's not very friendly," she said. "I really don't like her."

Arlie hadn't told Belinda about seeing Casey at the Sweeneys', or about their fight on the phone. Now, she said nothing. I don't like her, either, she thought. She couldn't blame Belinda. But it hurt to hear her say it, just the same.

"New kids are hard," Xenia said. "You always feel like they wish you were their old friends."

"She moves all over anyway," Belinda said, balling up her lunch bag. "Probably we'd get to know her and she'd just move again."

Xenia nodded. "Not worth it."

Arlie didn't say anything. "Don't let people tell you what's what," she heard Mr. Cunningham say.

This open mind thing was harder than it sounded.

That afternoon, alone in the apartment, Arlie picked up the phone and dialed 411. She'd never called Information before, but she knew how from seeing her mom do it. "Elliott Cunningham," she said to the man who answered. When the computerized voice gave the number, she wrote it down, then hung up the phone, feeling proud.

"Mr. Cunningham?" she said when he answered.

She didn't even have to say her name.

"*Arlie!* How are you?" he said, sounding genuinely happy to hear her voice.

"I'm okay," she said, and then, remembering to be polite, "How are *you?*"

"Very well, thank you. My joints have been acting up. That's the only thing."

"Don't they usually do that in the rain?" Arlie asked.

He laughed. "Well, well. So you've been *listening* when I talk to you!"

"I like that you can tell it's going to rain even if it isn't cloudy."

"Yeah, that's me. The human barometer." Mr. Cunningham sighed, as though it was a burden to have such a skill. "So. How's tricks?"

Mr. Cunningham always said that. It meant What's new?

"Not too much," Arlie said, feeling a little guilty. But she didn't want to tell him about her parents. She was tired of thinking about the car crash, Mom's coma, Casey Lane. Just the idea of trying to explain everything was exhausting. "We're coming to Leisure Valley. To do a play."

"So I've heard. What part are you?"

"I'm Petey. He's a boy, but I'm playing him anyway."

"Well, good for you."

"He's the hero," Arlie said. "He has the most lines."

"You good at memorizing?" Mr. Cunningham asked.

"Yeah. Memorizing is easy," Arlie said.

"I used to be good at memorizing. Now I can't even remember what year I was born." Mr. Cunningham sighed again, but he didn't really sound sad. "Youth. It's wasted on the young. You ever heard that before, Arlie?"

"I don't think so."

"Well, just enjoy being young: your good brain, the way your body works. That's all I'm saying."

Arlie knew he meant that you missed being young when you weren't anymore. "It's hard enjoying being Petey," she said.

"How come?"

"Well." She paused. "I know I should be having fun, being onstage, pretending to be someone else. Showing everyone in the audience what I learned, what I can do. But . . ."

"But what?" Sometimes Mr. Cunningham got impatient when people didn't talk fast enough.

"It's scary, too," she said.

"Oh. *That*." Mr. Cunningham said it as if he knew exactly what Arlie was talking about. "Yeah, acting's scary, all right."

"The thing is, how do you enjoy something that's so scary?" Arlie asked.

She held her breath, waiting for what Mr. Cunningham would say.

"Well, I've never been in a play before, Arlie," he said.

Her heart sank.

"But here's what I always say," Mr. Cunningham went on. "I always say there are two kinds of scary. There's good scary, and there's bad scary. Bad scary's if you're driving a hundred miles an hour on the freeway, or riding a bicycle without a helmet, or using a peashooter. Kids still have peashooters, Arlie?"

"I don't know. I never heard of them."

"I'm glad. You can put someone's eye out with a peashooter. Anyway, those things are bad scary. You want to stay away from bad scary."

"I always wear a helmet when I ride a bike."

"Good girl. Now, good scary's different. A different kettle of fish entirely."

Arlie loved the way Mr. Cunningham talked, with expressions no one else used anymore.

"Jumping off the high dive is good scary. So is raising your hand in class to answer a really tough question."

"I'm good at those things," Arlie said.

"I know you are."

"You're going to say that being in a play is good scary, right?"

Mr. Cunningham laughed. "Can't put one over on you, Arlie. That's why we're friends. We're both so smart."

"Smart's not brave," Arlie said, but she was flattered that he thought she was smart.

"You'll see," Mr. Cunningham said. "It'll be fine. You're gonna be great."

"'I miss my friends. I miss Grandma and Grandpa. I even miss the fruit stand.'" Arlie looked at Isabelle. "Is my voice shaking?"

"No," Isabelle said. She was sitting, legs crossed, at the kitchen table, a copy of *Who's Minding the Store?* on her lap. She was eating an apple. "Stop asking that. Your voice sounds fine."

"It feels like it's shaking," Arlie said.

"It sounds like always. Normal. Like you," Michael said from the couch. "You don't even sound like a boy."

"Yes, she does," Isabelle said, glancing over at him. "You have to use your imagination."

"Well, if I have to use my imagination, then why do you need costumes?" Michael asked. "Why can't I just *imagine* costumes?"

"You could," Isabelle said, "but that would be a different kind of play."

"Why can't I just imagine the whole play?" Michael asked. He was different since they had started talking to Dad on the phone. Grumpier. He argued more. Arlie

133

thought that talking to Dad made him aware that there was really something wrong with Mom.

"You can," Isabelle was saying. "Like a story in your head that you tell yourself."

Michael closed his eyes, then opened them. "Boring," he said. "*Who's Minding the Store?* is a boring play."

"No, it's not," Arlie said. But secretly she wondered if the only reason it wasn't boring to her was because she was in it.

"The thing about plays," Isabelle said. Then she paused. ". . . Without an audience, they're not very interesting. Even a little audience. Even just three people."

"What about two people?" Michael asked.

Isabelle ignored him.

"You need someone to share the experience with," she said. "Even strangers."

"I'm not supposed to talk to strangers," Michael said.

He's just arguing to argue, Arlie thought. Boy, is he a pain in the neck today.

"If you share an experience, maybe they're not strangers anymore," Isabelle said.

"Anyway, *this* audience isn't going to be strangers," Arlie said after a moment. "It's the people from Leisure Valley. Mr. Cunningham."

"Your friend," Isabelle said, remembering.

Arlie nodded. "The one who broke codes in World War II. And has a granddaughter who's an acrobat with the circus. She can tie herself in knots, Mr. Cunningham says."

Michael's eyes were wide.

"He says she looks like one of those balloon animals they make for little kids in the park," Arlie said. "Mr. Cunningham misses her when she's on tour. He says I remind him of her."

"Why?" Michael said. "You can't do anything like that."

"He just likes me." Arlie felt proud.

"With good reason," Isabelle said. "Try your lines again, so you can show Mr. Cunningham what a good actor you are."

It occurred to Arlie that she was going to have to perform in front of a real audience—grownups, not just her classmates. Real people, who would sit on the edge of their seats, waiting to see what would happen next. Waiting to see what she—Petey—would say.

Her throat felt like a hole that someone was shoveling sand into. But she took a breath and began her lines again, thinking that at the very least she wanted Isabelle and Mr. Cunningham to be proud of her.

"Casey Lane has left us," Mrs. Rubio said to the class on Wednesday morning.

"What?" Arlie asked.

"Her parents called the school this morning," Mrs. Rubio said. "It's an unexpected move."

The rest of the class listened without saying anything. Casey hadn't been around long enough to make much of a difference to anyone.

"Why?" Arlie asked. "Where? Where is she moving?"

"Please don't call out, Arlie," Mrs. Rubio said. "These things happen."

Warren raised his hand. "Who's going to be Charlie in the play?" he asked.

"Not a problem," Mrs. Rubio said. "One of the town folk can take two parts."

Slowly, Jeremy's hand inched up. "I'll do it," he said, sighing heavily, as though it was a great burden he was taking on.

Mrs. Rubio smiled at him. "Why, thank you, Jeremy," she said. She eyed the class. "See?" she said. "*No* one is irreplaceable."

All through Spelling and Language Arts, Arlie kept glancing over her shoulder, sneaking peeks at the empty desk behind her. She could almost believe that someone was sitting there; she was aware of a dim and floaty presence in the fleeting half second just before she turned her head. Someone or something: it made the little hairs on the back of her neck stand up, made her want to sit up straight.

A trick of the light, she knew. Something about the way the dust motes drifted downward in the slant of sunlight. Or maybe it was Mrs. Rubio passing the open window as she spoke, her shadow slithering over the desks and floor, not shaped like a woman, but somehow alive and breathing.

A trick of the light. Something.

ten

She could have just called. It would have been easier to call. Then she wouldn't have to look at her face, wouldn't have to watch her answer the questions Arlie would ask. But that would be chicken. The coward's way out. Arlie knew that.

As she stood on the front stoop, listening to the ring of the doorbell die away, she whispered, "Do yourself proud."

When Mrs. Sweeney opened the door, she looked surprised, but she kept smiling. "Hi, Arlie."

"Hi." Her heart beat; her stomach churned. She couldn't think through her fear. It was like being onstage, being Petey. And that was when it hit her: that what she was afraid of wasn't forgetting her lines, or tripping, or not knowing that she had toilet paper stuck to her shoe. It was that people wouldn't like her.

"How's your mom, sweetheart?" Mrs. Sweeney asked.

"The same," Arlie said. She was sick of people asking, sick of having to give the same answer. "My dad's better, though."

"I heard that," Mrs. Sweeney said. "I'm so glad."

"The doctors said we shouldn't go down until he's ready to leave the hospital," Arlie went on. "He's too weak to talk much. And he—they—don't look so good."

Mrs. Sweeney was nodding sympathetically.

"I—I just wanted to find out why you fired us," Arlie blurted out.

"Oh, well. It wasn't firing, exactly," Mrs. Sweeney said, taken aback. She had begun to wring her hands. She looked at Arlie and stopped. "Yes. Yes, it was. I'm sorry, Arlie."

From somewhere in the house, Arlie could hear Jesse shriek. Mrs. Sweeney looked over her shoulder, as though she was afraid she might see flames shooting out of the kitchen.

"Why?" Arlie asked.

Mrs. Sweeney looked back at Arlie and folded her arms over her chest. "Look, honey. Jesse's a handful. I know that. He's no dream date."

Arlie was surprised.

"He's a very headstrong little boy. Maybe too headstrong for most fifth graders."

Jesse shrieked again. Arlie couldn't tell if it was a happy shriek or a miserable shriek.

"I know you and Belinda did your best. And I really, really appreciate it. But some of the things Jesse said—"

"You should have fired just me," Arlie said. "Not Belinda. She was really good."

Mrs. Sweeney smiled. "You're a good friend, Arlie. But Jesse said some things. How Belinda was always feeding him cookies, trying to get him to do what she wanted. Jesse needs a firmer hand."

Casey's firm, Arlie thought. But that doesn't mean she's a better babysitter than Belinda.

"It made me realize that Belinda wasn't quite right for this job," Mrs. Sweeney said. "And I didn't want to fire just one of you. That wouldn't have been fair."

"I guess," Arlie said. "Did Jesse ever say anything about me?"

"Just that you were a lousy Chutes and Ladders player." Mrs. Sweeney smiled again. "He never likes his babysitters. And that's okay. I'm not looking for someone to be his friend."

Arlie took a deep breath. "How did you find out about Casey Lane?"

"Oh, her mom and I just started playing golf together. She mentioned that her daughter was very mature and responsible, and I thought it might be something nice for her, since she's new in the neighborhood."

"Did she ask you for this job?" Arlie asked.

Mrs. Sweeney hesitated. "No," she said at last. "I asked her. But when she said yes, I did ask if it would cause problems with you and Belinda. I didn't want to have anything to do with that," she added.

"What did she say?"

"That business was business. It was a funny thing for a little girl to say," Mrs. Sweeney said. "But she assured me that it wasn't a problem. That she would take care of it."

They heard another shriek.

"I'm sorry, Arlie. I've got to go." Mrs. Sweeney began to back away from the door. "Anything else?"

"No." Not here, anyway. "Thanks, Mrs. Sweeney." After a second, she added, "Tell Jesse I said hi."

But Mrs. Sweeney was already closing the door. From the expression on her face, Arlie could tell that she was trying to figure out which room all the broken things would be in.

She ran down the sidewalk: fast at first, then a little more slowly. She was afraid to walk, even though sweat dribbled down the hollow in the middle of her back and her chest felt as if it would explode. I should have come here first, she thought, rounding the last corner. For a second, she closed her eyes, hoping it wasn't too late.

When she opened them, she saw the moving van parked at the curb, its side doors open, a ramp leading down to the sidewalk. Three men were at the front door, easing a dolly loaded with boxes down the front steps. One of the men was shouting at the other two. Arlie could hear more shouting from inside the house.

She stood off to one side of the sidewalk as the men rolled the dolly down the front walk and up the ramp into the truck. Then she walked to the front door, which hung open. No one was around, and the movers weren't paying any attention to her. She stepped inside.

The front rooms were empty of furniture: they looked ghostly and abandoned, despite the shouts and thuds that could be heard from the rest of the house. "Casey?" she called, knowing that her voice was too soft to be heard over the din. She remembered Mrs. Rubio's instructions about projecting her voice and grew bolder. "Casey!" she called more loudly. When still no one responded, she walked down the hallway, toward Casey's open bedroom door. She heard bustling and voices and a radio switched to a hard-rock station. "Casey!" she called again.

At the threshold she stopped. The room was almost empty: the furniture had already been taken away. There were scraps of newspaper lying about, and things that looked as though they had collected dust under the bed: a plastic alien from a fast-food restaurant, a red comb, the blue top of a shampoo bottle. Even the drapes were gone.

Shoot, Arlie thought.

Then she heard a door open behind her in the hall. Before she could turn around, she heard Casey say, "What are you doing here?"

Arlie turned. Casey wore a blue dress and white flip-flops. Arlie had never seen her in flip-flops before: they looked out of place—sloppy and somehow too modern on her bony feet. Even though the day was warm and the atmosphere in the house chaotic, her hair was shiny and neat, her skin sweatless.

As if reading Arlie's thoughts, she smiled and gestured with her head. "It's complete bedlam," she said.

Arlie nodded, out of breath. "Wow," she said. "Moving again."

"I told you I never unpack."

"Where are you going?"

Casey shrugged. "I don't remember."

"Really? You don't remember? Really?"

"Mom said. I forget. Someplace with a beach."

Both girls shuffled around awkwardly, looking at the floor. It was a small measure of satisfaction to Arlie that Casey seemed to be feeling as uncomfortable as she was.

"I just went to the Sweeneys'," Arlie said. "I talked to Mrs. Sweeney."

Casey didn't say anything. She walked past Arlie into her room and knelt down, gathering the newspaper scraps and crumpling them into a ball.

Arlie said, "I'm sorry."

Casey didn't look up. "Sorry for what?"

"For saying you stole the job from Belinda and me. You didn't."

"I know I didn't."

"I shouldn't have said what I said. I shouldn't have jumped to conclusions."

Had she been doing that all along?

Still kneeling, Casey didn't move for a minute. Finally, she rose, her back still to Arlie. "Okay," she said.

Something about the way she didn't turn around made Arlie say, "You still shouldn't have done it."

Now Casey turned to look at her. "Done what?"

"Taken the job. It was ours, and it was important, and, and . . ."

"Arlie—"

"Don't say business is business," Arlie said. "You shouldn't have taken our job when you knew it was important to us."

After a minute Casey said, "I don't see it that way."

Case closed. That was that. You couldn't tell her anything, or change her mind, or make her see it a different way. Arlie realized sadly what the problem was: she just didn't like Casey Lane all that much.

But still. There was something. Wanting Casey to like *her*. An eerie foreboding that she would miss Casey when she was gone. The force of realizing this took Arlie by surprise, so that almost without meaning to, she said, "There's something else."

She met Casey's stare. "It's weird. It's kind of hard to say out loud."

"What?"

Those eyes: piercingly, shockingly blue. Who was in there? Arlie stared, trying to see, trying to really see.

"Come on. What?" Casey's tone was different; she couldn't cover up her curiosity.

Arlie thought of everything that had happened: the way her parents had left and Casey had mysteriously shown up, the inexplicable similarities, the weird coincidences. Would Bart Blodgett call these mysteries of the universe?

"You're the only person I told," she said, surprising herself again.

Casey nodded. "About the stage fright." She just said it; it wasn't a question.

"I didn't even tell Belinda, who's my best friend. Or Isabelle, who I love—" She stopped, choked up. "—love so much," she finished.

"I guess sometimes it's easier to tell someone you don't know very well," Casey said.

Arlie nodded. "Yes. That's it." She wiped her eyes with her hands, like a little kid. Like Jesse, she thought.

She had been going to tell Casey that she would miss her, but at the last minute she decided not to. She didn't feel like being so sentimental. She didn't even like Casey. She didn't want to bare her soul like that.

Her soul. The part of her that was inside, not part of her body, not an organ, not something a doctor could take a picture of, or give you pills for, or fix. The part of you that was really you: more than your face or your hands or your feet. Separate from your body, which needed food and rest and medicine; which could get hurt or injured or even die, but was just a big box, really, a container. A kind of house that you lived in for as long as you needed, until—what?

Her heart lurched.

Casey stood up. "I have to go," she said. "There's a lot more packing."

Arlie nodded, even though it looked like almost everything was all boxed up. "That's okay. I have to go, too."

Suddenly, it was all she could do not to run for the door. The old anxiety, the old sense of knowing, was back, biting at her insides. She had to get home. Something had happened.

Casey was standing at the bedroom door, like a gracious hostess saying goodbye.

"It was nice meeting you," she said formally, as if she had said it a hundred times before.

"Same," Arlie said. She walked past her, into the hall, frantic to get outside, to hit the sidewalk running. But first she turned around.

"Have fun in Santa Cruz," she said.

"What?" Casey said.

"It's pretty," Arlie said. "With beaches. And a board-walk."

"Hey!" Casey gripped the door frame. "How'd you know?"

Arlie smiled.

"You'll like it," she said. "Go to the beach once in a while. It's fun."

Casey looked stunned. Her mouth hung open, but she made no move to close it, or to speak.

Arlie turned and ran for the front door. She was going to yell out something about having a baby sister soon, but she stopped herself. She wanted Casey to think *she* was knowing and wise, for once; someone who didn't have to be told to speak more loudly or stand up straight. But she didn't want to scare her. She didn't want to be remembered as some kind of freak of nature.

She tore down the street, blood pulsing in her ears,

breath coursing through her lungs. She made herself not think about Casey. Run, she thought. Run. Just run. And then, as she rounded the corner of Isabelle's street, she had a new thought.

Please. Please, oh please, oh please.

And then she was at the front door of Isabelle's building, fumbling with her key, taking the stairs two at a time. Her heart beat so hard she thought it would burst. Just one more flight of stairs, she thought, and then the hallway, and then the door. And then I'll know.

But as she emerged from the stairwell, there was Isabelle in front of the apartment door, her face so lit up from smiling that the whole hallway seemed to shimmer, and Arlie stopped and smiled back, and that was when she knew that finally, everything really was going to be all right.

eleven

On Thursday morning, everyone from Room 22 was talking so wildly that they didn't even hear the eight-thirty bell ring. Mrs. Rubio was more dressed up than usual. She was wearing lipstick and a jacket that matched her pants. She was also yelling her head off. Preplay jitters, Arlie thought. Her stomach jumped as though she were on a roller coaster.

"Props, people, props!" Mrs. Rubio cried, checking her list. "We need to collect all the props. Nothing can be left behind. Come on now! We need crates! We need plastic fruit! We need the street sign!"

Some of the moms and dads had cleaned out their garages in hopes of finding things Mrs. Rubio and the class could use. Mr. Sanchez had painted a street sign and donated hats and a pitchfork. Maybe to make up for Jeremy always being so bad, Arlie thought.

Everyone was searching desks and the classroom cupboards for plastic fruit. Belinda rummaged in her backpack. "I can't find my reading glasses," she moaned.

"Hey," Arlie said. "You sound just like a grandma." She watched as Belinda tore through crumpled math worksheets and a crushed, unopened bag of cheese curls. "Are you nervous?"

"Not too much. Mrs. Blythe will be there."

Mrs. Blythe was Belinda's special friend at Leisure Valley. Belinda read her books about the ocean. Mrs. Blythe was blind, but back when she could see and was about forty years younger, she had been a lifeguard at Sandy Point. "When you read, it's like I can smell salt in the air," she was always telling Belinda.

"Are you scared?" Belinda asked.

"No," Arlie said.

"Because you look scared," Belinda said. "You've looked scared the whole time."

"What do you mean 'the whole time'?"

Belinda said gently, "Since you got the part."

When Arlie didn't say anything, Belinda touched her arm. "Why didn't you tell me?"

Arlie looked over her shoulder, but everyone was too busy collecting props to be paying any attention to them. "Because," she said, "it's embarrassing."

"Not to me," Belinda said. "I'm always telling you when I'm afraid."

Arlie remembered having to leave a night-light on during sleepovers, having to leave the Fourth of July picnic before it got dark. "I don't know," she said. "It's just harder for me."

"It shouldn't be," Belinda said. "Friends should tell each other stuff."

Arlie thought about telling her to stop saying "should," but she didn't. Maybe Belinda was right.

"I'm sorry," she whispered.

"My mom always says to just picture people in their underwear."

"My dad says that, too." It never helped. She didn't want

to think about Mr. Cunningham and Mrs. Blythe in their underwear. "Parents are so weird."

They both laughed.

Belinda said, "I'm glad about your mom not being in a coma anymore."

"I know," Arlie said. "Me, too."

"It's too bad she can't come to the play."

Arlie nodded, even though she wasn't sure she really wanted her mother in the audience, watching her, mouthing *Stand up straight* when she thought she had caught Arlie's eye. "After the show, Isabelle's going to come get us and we're going to drive down to the hospital to see them."

"How long will you be gone?" Belinda asked.

"Just until Monday."

"Good," she said. "I'd miss you if it was longer."

Behind them, Curtis Little was raising his hand and yelling for Mrs. Rubio.

"What is it, Curtis?" Mrs. Rubio asked.

"Eduardo has arm dandruff," Curtis said.

Mrs. Rubio slammed a book down on her desk. It scared everyone into silence.

"Now, look. I need everyone to quiet down and get serious. I don't want to hear about missing street signs or smashed-in fruit or . . . arm dandruff. Or anything."

No one said a word.

"I want you to bring any remaining props up to my desk. We'll load them into these garbage bags. Then I want you to head out to the bus. Take a garbage bag with you. And take your scripts," she said, her voice beginning to rise as everyone started to talk again. "You can look them over one last time on the ride to Leisure Valley."

Arlie gathered up her script, knowing she wouldn't look at it: she'd known her lines for weeks. Her heart was slamming around in her chest, but she felt better than she'd thought she would. It was nice to have told Belinda, nice that now, at least, her best friend knew how she really felt.

They pulled onto Leisure Valley Parkway about an hour later. The uniformed man at the gate waved them through, then continued to wave as the kids, mostly the boys, waved wildly back. Boys are so dumb, Arlie thought. You'd think no one had ever waved to them before.

Leisure Valley was like a town within a town. Most of the people who lived there played golf, so there was a big golf course with houses all around it. Mr. Cunningham hated golf. He told Arlie that no one liked it, that what everyone really liked was riding around in the little golf carts. His shiny blue eyes crinkled, letting Arlie know that he was kidding and not kidding at the same time. He explained how the management at Leisure Valley had taken his cart away because he was always driving into people's backyards by mistake. "They called me a menace to public safety," he said, looking happy. When Arlie laughed, he said, "Sometime when I know you're coming, I'll steal one and take you for a spin."

"Then you'll really be a menace," Arlie said.

"Why live to be eighty-four if you can't get people all riled up?" Mr. Cunningham had answered, smiling his biggest smile.

The bus slowed and turned into the community center parking lot, which was already beginning to fill. As the class trooped off the bus and waited for the driver and Mrs. Rubio to hand out the garbage bags full of props, Arlie noticed a hand-lettered sign posted on the bulletin board by the front entrance: COME SEE SPRINGHILL VALLEY FIFTH GRADERS IN "WHO'S MINDING THE STORE?" REFRESHMENTS AFTER.

We're celebrities, Arlie thought, and for once, her stomach didn't churn. She found herself wondering if all the seats would be taken, and if Mr. Cunningham would get there early.

The community center was like a little school, with classrooms off a main hallway. Arlie had seen bulletin-board postings for things like Cooking with Woks Made Easy and Financial Planning for Seniors. Once, she had peeked into a classroom to see if it looked like hers. Except for a blackboard and desks, it didn't. No student artwork on the walls, or maps of the world that rolled down.

At the end of the corridor was the center's main hall. It was a big room with plain, white walls and a metal clock that was always ten minutes too fast. Here, Leisure Valley residents—mostly "the gals," as Mr. Cunningham called them—took classes like Line Dancing and Fabulous Fitness Through T'ai Chi. There was also a stage, a real stage, with green velvet curtains that opened and closed when a gold-braided tassled rope was pulled. The last time the class had visited Leisure Valley, Mr. Cunningham had taken Arlie backstage and shown her around. She'd liked the old sets the best. Whenever the residents put on a play themselves, they kept the sets they'd designed. They were like paintings on very large wooden canvases: Arlie had especially liked the sets from a long-ago production of *My Fair Lady*. In one, ladies in fancy, old-fashioned dresses and hats were looking at something with binoculars. Mr. Cunningham said it was racehorses.

Now Mrs. Rubio led the class through a doorway off to one side of the stage. Everyone trooped up a short stairway. The light backstage glowed dimly, casting shadows over the old sets and other things Arlie had missed when she had been there before: ancient brushes and cans of paint, trays full of hammers and screwdrivers, a wedding veil perched atop a coat rack, a pair of dusty basketballs, a scarred wooden coffee table covered with dust.

"Please don't touch anything," Mrs. Rubio said, her voice a well-heard whisper. "These things belong to Leisure Valley. Leave them alone." Mrs. Rubio pushed a stray strand of hair back over her forehead. She looked sweaty.

Maybe it was the magical aura of being backstage: the feeble light; the odd assortment of props—basketballs, wedding veils—that didn't seem to go with anything else; the sense of things being built and torn down, of things stored away until they became useful and necessary again. Strangely, amazingly, Room 22 got busy unpacking props and arranging furniture on the stage. Nobody yelled, nobody punched anybody, nobody cried or made disparaging remarks about unzipped zippers or arm dandruff or nose hair or warts.

A miracle, Arlie thought, helping Warren and Xenia carry crates of plastic pears to stage left. Or magic, or something. A mystery. Something you could see and hear but not explain.

Maybe, she thought, the world was full of magic: little pieces of it, like bits of glass on a sandy beach that looked like nothing—rocks or driftwood—most of the time. But once in a while the sunlight caught and held one, and it glittered, and you saw it and knew for sure what it was, and that it was really there.

She thought the same thing an hour and fifteen minutes later as she stood onstage, in the scene where the innkeeper told Petey that all her rooms were full.

It was the moment when Arlie first realized that she wasn't thinking about her pounding heart; that her skin wasn't clammy and her mind wasn't racing in blind, numb terror. It was the moment *after* the moment when she forgot—truly forgot—that she was Arlie Metcalfe. For *that* fleeting instant, she felt like Petey, a boy who slouched, who knew in his bones what it felt like to have left everything behind, to have nowhere to sleep. For that moment, the fear Arlie felt was the fear of having nowhere to go and no place to call home. It was Petey's fear, not hers.

Later, when she and the rest of Room 22 were bowing before the clapping, cheering crowd, she knew she wanted to experience this feeling again and again, forever. Not the pride she felt in having done a good job or conquering her fears. A different feeling, hard to explain. By being Petey, she finally knew who *she* really was.

It was as if her soul was flying.

"Brava! Brava!" Mr. Cunningham called, clapping his knobby hands over his head as she approached him at the punch bowl.

Arlie blushed with pleasure.

"Hi, Mr. Cunningham," she said.

He was flanked by Mrs. Snodgrass and a lady who liked to be called Grandma Betty. Mrs. Snodgrass used to be a school principal. She liked to talk about the rumors that she'd kept dead kids in a utility closet in the teachers' lounge: she had started those rumors herself, she said, to keep the trouble-makers in line. Grandma Betty was six feet tall and wore blue jeans and big boots, like the men who climbed telephone poles. She had fourteen grandchildren and wanted more. "I can always use more," she would say with a wink, as though she wanted them to mow her lawn and fix things around the house.

"What a good job you did," Mrs. Snodgrass said. "All those lines!"

"One hundred and forty-three," Arlie said.

"My, my," Grandma Betty said. "I can barely remember my own telephone number."

Mr. Cunningham cocked his head in Arlie's direction. "This one's sharp," he said. "That's why she's the star."

Arlie helped herself to a sugar cookie. It was embarrassing to be the object of so much attention, but pleasant, too.

"You did such a good job," Mrs. Snodgrass said to her. "So many lines to memorize!"

"Sometimes I have to look at an envelope addressed to me to remember where I live," Grandma Betty said.

The adults laughed. Arlie wanted to, but she thought it might be rude.

"That young man—the grandfather—what was his name?" Grandma Betty asked Arlie.

"Warren Rutherford."

"Now, he was very good," Grandma Betty said. "I could hear every word he said."

"He was yelling, though," Mr. Cunningham said. "What the heck was he yelling for?"

Arlie loved that Mr. Cunningham didn't try to talk politely just because kids were around. "Warren's just like that," she said.

"He didn't think we were all deaf, did he?" Mr. Cunningham asked. Sometimes he got touchy about being old.

"Oh, no," Arlie said. "He yelled all the way through rehearsals."

"He's got skinny knees," Mr. Cunningham said, but not to be mean. Old people often just said what they thought, Arlie had learned. You weren't supposed to get offended.

"And big skinny feet," she added, wiping sugar cookie crumbs from her mouth.

The women laughed and excused themselves, making their way to a dignified man who was sitting in a wheelchair near the brownies.

"That cagey ole Ed Smaker," Mr. Cunningham said in a low, disapproving voice to Arlie. "He doesn't really need that wheelchair, you know."

Arlie nodded, watching as Grandma Betty arranged brownies and cookies on a plate and took it to Mr. Smaker.

"Not a darn thing wrong with his legs," Mr. Cunningham said. "He just does it to get the girls."

"And the brownies," Arlie said, watching Mr. Smaker smile at Grandma Betty.

Mr. Cunningham laughed. "Hey, Arlie," he said, catching his breath. "You were good."

He was really looking at her. He wasn't just saying it to be nice.

"Thanks," she said.

They chewed their cookies in silence for a moment as the room buzzed around them. Arlie saw Warren and Jeremy at a table with Belinda and Mrs. Blythe. Under the table, Mrs.

Blythe's yellow Labrador retriever wearing its SERVICE DOG sweater lay with its nose on its paws. Jeremy kept leaning down to pet it, not even looking embarrassed for doing something nice. Across the room, Mrs. Rubio stood at the center of a small crowd of people. Arlie could tell by the way she kept flinging her arm that she was showing them something she'd learned in her fly-fishing class.

"Hey, Mr. Cunningham," she said.

"Yeah, doll, what?"

"Do you believe in magic?"

"Well, now." Mr. Cunningham swallowed the last of his cookie. "I'm pretty careful about that word 'magic.'"

Arlie sighed. Why couldn't she get a straight answer?

"Magic makes folks think of wands and rabbits in top hats," Mr. Cunningham said.

"Not that kind of magic," Arlie said.

"I've been around a long time," Mr. Cunningham said. "I've seen a lot of things that *look* like magic. I've got no other explanation for 'em, so I guess that's what it was."

"Oh," Arlie said. She was disappointed. She wanted proof.

Mr. Cunningham smiled. "I'm gonna tell you a story, Arlie." He paused. "You know I got breathing troubles, right?"

Arlie nodded. Mr. Cunningham used to smoke cigarettes, before he knew they were bad for you. He was always having to use an inhaler and take pills.

"Well, once, years ago, my wife and I went on a little trip. Drove up to Mendocino for a long weekend. It was pretty. Winding roads and fog. Beverly liked the views." Mr. Cunningham pursed his lips and looked down at his feet for a minute, the way he always did when he talked about his dead wife. Then he looked up again. "Real pretty," he said.

"Mendocino's where my mom and dad went for their honeymoon," Arlie said. "Mom got carsick and threw up the whole way there."

Mr. Cunningham laughed. "Yep. It's twisty, all right. Anyway, Beverly and I got all the way up to Mendocino and found the house we were staying in. It belonged to someone else, a doctor, and he rented it out on weekends. Pretty house. It had a hot tub outside."

"I love all that swirly water," Arlie said.

Mr. Cunningham nodded. "So I opened the trunk to get our bags, and only Beverly's was in there." Mr. Cunningham shook his head. "I blamed her and she blamed me. We yelled about it." He blinked hard and pursed his lips again. "I wasn't an easy man," he said.

Arlie wanted to say "It's all right," but she didn't know how, to someone so old. So she just listened.

"My suitcase had my inhaler and all my pills. So here I was up in the middle of nowhere, without my stuff. And this wasn't stuff you could just walk into a pharmacy and buy," Mr. Cunningham said. "You had to get a doctor to call in your prescriptions. And it was eight o'clock on a Friday night." He shook his head again. "In the middle of nowhere."

He sighed. "Anyway, we go inside the house, and I'm thinking, I've got to call a doctor or a hospital up here. Someone who can get me my medicine. The phone was on a little end table in the bedroom. The kind with a drawer that looked about the right size to hold a phone book. So I opened the drawer, thinking I'd look up the name of the nearest hospital and see if someone there could help me."

He paused and looked right at her. "It was the most

amazing thing, Arlie. I pulled open that drawer, looking for the phone book, and it was full—*full*—of unopened inhalers. Crammed full." He shook his head again, in wonder. "There must have been thirty of them. Brand-new."

"Wow," Arlie said.

"I took one, of course. I was already starting to wheeze. Just knowing I didn't have my pills was enough to make me short of breath."

"I'm short of breath just listening to you," Arlie said.

Mr. Cunningham laughed. "I left the doc a note, and money to pay for the inhaler. Didn't want to just make off with it." He fell silent for a minute, then looked again at Arlie. "Now, you can tell me that the reason all those inhalers were in that drawer was because that doctor had asthma. Or maybe he was a doctor who had a lot of patients with asthma. Or maybe the last renter at the house had asthma, and left all *his* inhalers."

"That doesn't sound like it would be it," Arlie said.

"Nothing explains it," Mr. Cunningham said. "Nothing explains why I opened that drawer, or why those inhalers were in there. Beverly said it was just a coincidence. She was like that. She liked to think there was a logical reason for everything."

Arlie nodded.

Mr. Cunningham leaned in close. "You can't tell me that wasn't *something*," he whispered. "Not magic. But *something*."

She wanted to tell him everything, but she didn't. It would be like trying to outdo his story. Instead, she said, "I know."

Mr. Cunningham looked satisfied with that. "I told Beverly, You can't always *know* everything." Then he whispered, "Sometimes we're not *supposed* to know."

Arlie said, "It's not a test."

Mr. Cunningham nodded in agreement. "That's right."

"Maybe you're not supposed to figure it out," Arlie said. "Maybe things like that happen to teach you that you *can't* know everything."

"Hey," Mr. Cunningham said. "I like that." After a minute he said, "Beverly never did want to believe that."

"I believe it," Arlie said.

"Well, good for you." Mr. Cunningham pulled another cookie off the tray. "How'd you get so smart?"

"It doesn't feel smart," Arlie said. "It just feels true."

twelve

The next day was Friday. Room 22 performed *Who's Minding the Store?* for the parents in the Multipurpose Room. It wasn't as good as the community center at Leisure Valley—there wasn't a stage, and everything echoed; the parents had to sit on lunch-table benches that weren't comfortable; and everything smelled like bologna. But at the end, everyone clapped and smiled. Arlie saw Isabelle beaming in the front row and thought how it was nice to have someone there just for her.

Her heart thudded, her palms sweated, her brain went fuzzy and blank. But somehow it wasn't as bad the second time. She knew it would fade eventually and she'd be left with that feeling again, the thrill of being herself, her soul flying. The good scary stuff was worth it, in the end.

After the performance and cookies in Room 22, Arlie left school early. Mrs. Rubio put her arm around Arlie's shoulders and told her she was happy for her and not to worry about missing science: they were just going to look at pictures of sepals and stamens. Belinda hugged her and whispered, "Awesome!" and then, "You're going to be the next Rulia Joberts!" The weirdest thing was Jeremy Sanchez, his mouth full of Rice Krispies Treats, giving her a thumbs-up as she headed for the door. He had looked over both shoulders to make sure no one was watching, and Arlie knew she wasn't supposed to respond in any way. Pretending not to see was what he wanted her to do, and what she did, but there was a flutter in her stomach, the way it felt when someone who usually didn't notice you thought you had done a good job.

The drive to Paso Robles was long and slow, through San Jose and Gilroy (THE GARLIC CAPITAL OF THE WORLD, the billboard said), past turnoffs for Monterey and Carmel and Gonzales. The oak trees along the freeway were thick with leaves that looked dry and papery under the warm spring sun. Isabelle played Frank Sinatra Christmas songs on a tape recorder in the front seat until the batteries ran out. When Michael asked her why her car didn't have a CD player, her eyes got huge. "Cars have CD players?" she asked.

They arrived at the hospital around five o'clock. Looking up at the big building, Arlie felt afraid again. "Maybe we should go to the motel first," she said.

"No," Isabelle said, unusually definitive. "We'll go later. After."

"Am I gonna have to get a shot?" Michael whined. He hated doctors and hospitals. As a toddler, he had gotten a lot of ear infections, and he'd broken his collarbone when he was four.

"You don't have to do anything," Arlie said. "Just be there. Just behave. Don't knock over any machines or spill any pills or run into anything."

Michael never had to do anything. He just had to show up, and that was enough. But Arlie—Arlie could do everything right and it wouldn't matter. It wasn't fair, she thought, feeling the old surge of resentment underneath her fear. It had been that way all her life, and it wasn't fair at all.

But as they walked from the parking garage into the main

atrium, Michael reached for her hand, and some of her anger melted away as she felt him grip her tightly. It wasn't fair, but it wasn't Michael's fault. He couldn't help it if their mother loved him more.

They both followed Isabelle, who was walking purposefully toward a bank of elevators, this time not needing to ask at the information desk where to go. Inside the elevator, she pressed three. They stood together, watching the numbers light up over the doors, not meeting each others' eyes or knowing what to say. Isabelle bit her lip and tapped her foot. It occurred to Arlie that Isabelle was going to see her sister, that she had her own feelings and fears about everything that had happened but she had kept them to herself.

When the doors opened, Arlie and Michael followed Isabelle, her boot heels clicking on the linoleum floor, down the hall, past rooms with other people in them. Most of the sick people—the ones in beds—were old, but a couple might have been the same age as Arlie's parents. What did they do with all the sick kids? She tried to imagine being sick in a hospital and couldn't.

"What's that smell?" Michael whispered.

"That's just how it is in hospitals," Arlie said, trying to cover up her own distaste.

Isabelle stopped before a door left partly ajar. She turned and knelt down so she was on Michael's level, but Arlie knew she was talking to both of them.

"Okay, you guys. Listen up. They're going to look weird. Not quite like they always do. Weak and pale and maybe a little thin. Your mom's still got some tubes in her."

Michael's eyes were huge with terror.

"So take a deep breath and be brave," Isabelle said.

Michael's eyes narrowed. "I'm brave!" he said.

Arlie thought, Am I? She didn't know. She used to think so, compared to Belinda. Now she wasn't sure. It seemed as though she'd been afraid an awful lot lately.

"Being brave doesn't mean not crying," Isabelle said. "You can cry. You can do or say whatever you feel."

"I'm not gonna cry," Michael said. "I never cry."

Isabelle rose. "Okay," she said. "Here we go." As if they were on the Grizzly at Great America and the car had just lurched forward, up the first hill.

Isabelle pulled the door open and held it for Arlie and Michael. The room was bright: the curtains at the window had been drawn back. Arlie could see the yellow hills in the distance, dotted with leafy trees. She thought how glad she was that her mother had a pretty view to look at. Everything in her body was hammering at once.

First she saw her father, sitting upright in a chair. He looked almost the same. Arlie felt a caving-in of relief: Isabelle's words had scared her. But Dad looked like himself, just thinner, like Isabelle had said, and a little bruised. He had a cut on his cheek that looked as though it had been worse before. Arlie was glad she hadn't seen it then.

Michael burst into tears.

"Oh, sweetie," Dad said, holding out his arms, not trying to stand up, Arlie noticed.

Michael ran blindly to their father and threw his arms around his neck.

"It's okay, Michael," Dad said, closing his eyes and smiling as he hugged Michael back. "It's okay."

Arlie realized her eyes were glued to them. She couldn't look toward the beds.

Michael sobbed and sobbed. Dad patted his back and rocked him from side to side. He'd finally stopped saying "It's okay." He just kept rocking and patting and hugging with his eyes closed. Arlie stood there, arms dangling at her sides, waiting for her father to open his eyes and notice her. She was aware of Isabelle behind her, bending over one of the beds. She felt as if she was at a party and didn't know anyone.

"Arlie," Isabelle said.

Taking a deep breath, she turned. There she was, her mother, almost lost beneath the bedclothes, smiling feebly, Isabelle's hand on her shoulder. She wore a hospital gown speckled with blue flowers and edged in blue trim. The kind of thing she hated, Arlie thought. Her mother was partial to dark colors without prints. The sight of her neck, pale and bony, propped against the thin pillow, was shocking. Arlie felt an urge to tug the sheet up high so that it would hide her mother's skin, but she couldn't move. She was hit with such a rush of relief and gratitude that she thought it would knock her over.

And love. For her mom, who took care of her, and kept her out of danger, and watched out for her. Who never lied, who could be counted on, no matter what. All things Arlie didn't think about much, or took for granted. Usually, she was so hurt and angry that she forgot about everything her mother did that made her feel safe and, in a funny way, treasured.

"Arlie," Isabelle said again, holding out her other hand. "Come close. It's okay."

Then Arlie did go close. She felt no urge to cry. Mom would hate it if she cried. She concentrated on her mother's neck, which had become easier to look at than her face. It was the face she remembered, the face she knew, but it was pale and sunken and somehow changed, as though someone had rearranged its bones. She couldn't look at her eyes yet.

"Hi, Arlie," her mother said. The same voice, but thinner, as if underwater. More relief, to hear it.

"Hi," she said back.

"I'm sorry," her mother said. And then more, about looking the way she did, about not being able to sit up, or talk louder, but Arlie didn't hear, because the shock of hearing her mother say "I'm sorry" was like water rushing over her, so that she had to struggle to take in air.

"It's okay," Arlie said, and then there was more silence.

"Hey, pumpkin," she heard her dad say behind her. She turned away from the bed. He had finally let go of Michael, who still stood close, his hand resting on their father's hospital-gowned thigh. Arlie approached him, trying to smile.

"It's okay," Dad said as she hugged him gingerly. "I won't break."

"I know," she said, her voice a whisper. She wanted to say what she felt, let the words out in a rush, but she held on to them, afraid to hear them. They might sound silly and not come out the way she meant them to. Better just to hug and keep everything inside.

When she pulled away from her dad, she touched one of his hands. The index finger was wrapped in gauze, kept straight by a metal splint. She met his eyes, and he laughed, knowing that she was worried about how he would hold his drumsticks.

"Just like your mother," he said fondly, but it chilled her a little, washed away a little of the gladness.

"Michael," Isabelle said from the bed, "come here and say hi to your mom."

Michael rubbed his eye with one fist, a little boy again, pouty and mad.

"It's okay, Isabelle," she heard her mother say. "He can't."

The way she said it. As though she wasn't at all surprised. Maybe, Arlie thought, that was why her mom always seemed to be nicer to Michael, to like him more. Maybe she just cut him more slack, because she thought he needed it.

Arlie said to Dad, "Is this your room, too?"

"As of yesterday," he said. "I had a room on another floor, until your mom . . ." He let the sentence dangle. "But the nurses are great. They moved me in so your mom can keep an eye on me."

He looked so relieved.

"Arlie," her mother said weakly from the bed, "tell me what's been going on."

Arlie let go of her father's hand and approached the bed again. It was strange and exciting to have her mother single her out, take an interest in her, when Michael was standing right there. "Well, there was a play at school. A real play. And I got the lead."

Her mother closed her eyes slowly, then slowly opened them. It was her way of nodding, Arlie could tell.

"It was yesterday and today." Was it really just this morning that she had been Petey in the Multipurpose Room? "And I played the main character. A boy. Petey."

Again her mother blinked. A smile played at her lips, which looked thin and dry.

"I was good," Arlie said.

After a minute, her mother said, "Did you remember all your lines?"

Arlie nodded. "Except for two times. I made something up that fit in with what everyone else was saying. That's what Mrs. Rubio said to do."

"A good actress should remember her lines," her mother said.

"I *was* good," Arlie said, more forcefully this time.

Her mother set her head back down on the pillow as Isabelle replaced the water on the bedside table. "I never said you weren't," she whispered.

You never said I was, Arlie thought, thinking of Casey.

Then she remembered that it was because of Casey that she'd even tried out for Petey in the first place. That if Casey hadn't tried out for Charlie, Arlie would never have thought to try out for Petey. She would have been too afraid in front of Jeremy and the others, being the only girl trying out for a boy part.

In a weird way, Casey had made her brave.

"I'm not going to take Architectural Drawing this summer," Arlie said. "I'm going to save up for acting classes. I talked to Mrs. Rubio, and she said I should take them." She paused. "She *said* I should."

Mom licked her lips and faintly asked for more water. Ignoring what she'd said. Letting Arlie know that Mrs. Rubio didn't know what she was talking about, that acting classes weren't important. Or maybe that actresses didn't make very much money, and had to work as waitresses and drive broken-down cars until they got discovered. Or that Arlie was just a lost cause, a screwup, a mess who didn't know *what* she wanted. Someone who couldn't decide between being an architect and being an actress would eventually make the wrong decision anyway.

Then the strangest thing happened. "Good for you," Mom said.

Arlie was stunned.

She couldn't remember her mother ever having talked to her this way before. Thoughts crowded her brain—things she had wanted to tell her mother while she'd been sick, and other things, too, that she thought she'd forgotten: how a long time ago she had wanted to be a ballerina; how she wished they could have a cat.

Her mother closed her eyes. Arlie waited for her to open them, but she didn't.

She looked at Isabelle, who put her finger to her lips. "Asleep," she whispered.

No! Arlie screamed inside her head. *Wake up! You can't start saying nice things and then run out of strength!*

"Be patient," Isabelle whispered. "There's time."

Their eyes met, Arlie's full of questions.

"I know," Isabelle said, smiling. "Amazing."

She put her hands on Arlie's shoulders and gently pushed her away from the bed, toward the chair her dad sat in. "Come on, Dave. How about you get back in bed while we settle in across the street?"

Dad nodded gratefully. "I wouldn't mind a catnap," he said, as though he could take it or leave it. A lie, Arlie thought, looking at his pale skin, his drooping eyelids.

Isabelle helped him over to his bed. He sat on it carefully, like Mr. Cunningham with no energy. Arlie could tell that he couldn't wait to lie down. She bit her lip, watching as he slowly hoisted his skinny legs up onto the mattress. Her father had never had skinny legs before.

Impulsively she went to him and leaned down to hug

him. This time, she really hugged. "You said you wouldn't break," she whispered.

He hugged her back. "No chance," he said.

Later, in the motel room, unable to contain herself, Arlie said to Isabelle, "What do *you* think happened?"

Isabelle smiled as she unfolded a blouse and went to hang it in the closet, stepping over Michael, who was playing on the floor. "Something very nice."

More than nice. "Bart Blodgett would have had a stroke," Arlie said.

Isabelle turned away from the closet and looked at her. "She isn't a monster, bunny."

"I know that. But you've got to admit, she doesn't usually say stuff like that to me."

Isabelle picked up another blouse. "Maybe she's changed. That happens sometimes. People get sick or hurt and see things in a new way."

"Do you think that's what happened?"

"I don't know," Isabelle said. She looked fondly at Arlie. "Don't get your hopes too high. People are who they are."

"But they can change. You just said."

"Not everything. Not all at once."

Arlie sighed. Part of her knew Isabelle was right. But what about male sea horses? What about Mr. Cunningham's inhalers? Things you couldn't explain. "Maybe just this one time," she said.

After a moment, Isabelle said, "Don't be too disappointed. That's all."

Being disappointed made Arlie think of something that had been bothering her. "I didn't like her very much," she said.

"Who?"

"Casey." My mom, she thought.

"Well," Isabelle said. "You can't like everyone."

"I guess so."

"But I'll bet if you thought really hard, you'd be able to come up with a couple of things about Casey that you *did* like," Isabelle said.

Was this true? After a moment, Arlie said, "The way she made me work harder on the play. I didn't like it when she was doing it, but she made me try harder. It made me a better Petey."

"You have *friends,* and you have *family,*" Isabelle said, her palms upturned in front of her, as if she held things of similar weight in each one. "Friends are special because you get to pick them."

If Casey still went to my school, Arlie thought, I wouldn't pick her.

From under the bed, Michael said, "There's gross stuff under here."

"And no matter how infuriating the people in your family are," Isabelle said, "somehow, no matter what, you always love them."

"If I find a comb under here, can I use it?" Michael asked.

"Under no circumstances," Isabelle said, not taking her eyes off Arlie. "Not that you don't love your friends," she added.

"In a different way," Arlie said.

Isabelle turned back to her unpacking. "Now you're getting it," she said.

She fumbled with something underneath a nightgown. "So. An actress, huh?"

Arlie smiled. "Maybe."

"What about being an architect?" Isabelle asked, but not like Mom would have. She was just curious.

"Well, I like that, too. Making houses. Thinking of people who'll live there. But—" She wanted to explain about the flying feeling and couldn't. If she said the words out loud, they wouldn't be right.

"Well, someone has to make the sets for plays. Did you ever think of that?" Isabelle asked.

"No," Arlie said. "I didn't."

"Maybe you'll be a set designer."

"Maybe," Arlie said, even though she didn't think she'd get that flying feeling designing sets. But it did sound fun.

"Or maybe you'll be a physicist," Isabelle said.

She had no idea what that was. "It doesn't sound like something I'd like," she said.

"My point," Isabelle said, "is that you don't have to know when you're eleven. Anything is possible."

Arlie smiled again. Another thing she didn't have to know. The world was full of them. Wonderful.

Isabelle turned back to her suitcase. "Hey. I almost forgot."

She held a small box wrapped in twine and plain brown paper.

"It came in the mail for you today," Isabelle said. "I threw it in my bag on my way out the door."

Arlie took the box and began to pull off the twine. She didn't recognize the handwriting, and there was no return address. It didn't matter. She knew who had sent it.

She took the lid carefully off the unwrapped box and peeled back a thin layer of tissue paper. Nestled in more tissue was a fish made of clear glass, with what looked like globs of orange marmalade suspended within its body. Its eyes and mouth were painted on in black, and it was attached to a base made to resemble part of the ocean floor.

"She never gave them away," Isabelle breathed, peering into the box. Then she looked at Arlie. "Remember? I told you."

Gingerly, Arlie brought the fish out of the box. Pinching it between her thumb and first finger, she held it up to the light. "It sparkles," she said.

"They catch the light," Isabelle said. "I used to sit in front of hers. She kept them on a windowsill so the sun would shine through them."

Arlie turned the fish over. There it was: "C.L." in tiny, delicate letters carved into the bottom of the pedestal.

"Amazing," Isabelle said.

Arlie smiled and nodded as she gently set the fish back in the tissue paper and closed the lid.

"You're going to have to dust it," Isabelle said. "She'll go crazy if you don't dust it."

"I know," Arlie said. "I don't mind."

And amazingly, she didn't.